THE MAN FROM THE MIST

P. J. Mann

Copyright © 2020 P. J. Mann

All rights reserved.

ISBN: 978-952-69294-7-7

ACKNOWLEDGMENTS

A special thanks goes to my editor Tricia Drammeh, who went through the whole documents to make it shine, and it's indeed shining. My followers, friends and subscribers for their continuous encouragement.

CHAPTER 1

Dave averted his eyes from the computer screen, and for the first time in hours, he glanced outside the window as the sun started to set.

A long exhale accompanied by a whine filled the silence of the room.

Despite the tiredness weighing on his eyelids, he couldn't take any break. It was one of those evenings when Dave had to work longer than the usual seven hours.

The editing job at the newspaper wasn't what he'd been dreaming of. Still, he had accustomed himself to it, like he'd had to accept the many defeats he'd suffered over his lifetime.

Dave's existence balanced well on a grayscale; nothing noteworthy ever happened in his life, and no particular social events ever occurred.

He spent most of his life in anonymity, ignored by the majority of the people, not appreciated by the few others who did know him.

Being shy and introverted wasn't all; nature gave him an extra challenge to overcome – invisibility.

Now, he knew he wasn't invisible in the literal sense of the word, but everybody could tell the difference when Joseph, the reporter who covered the sports section, or Sally, fashion and lifestyle columnist, came to the breakroom for coffee and the times when he did.

When they came in, everybody turned to greet them, asking questions, advice, or wanting to chat with them.

In response, they tossed a great joke to make people laugh, particularly Joseph, with his irresistible charisma, able to attract attention by coming inside a room.

For Dave, it was completely different. Nobody even acknowledged his presence.

Many times, he stayed on the sidelines, watching Joseph and fantasizing what it would be like to be like him.

Yet, every time, he remained in his corner, unable to find the courage to be as social and charming as they were.

Like a figure in the mist, he was one of those faded silhouettes crossing you during the foggy days.

They don't have a face, expression, or clothing style; they're only shadows, just like him. A chilly, light rain was falling on that mid-October evening.

Tiny drops of ice water hit his skin with the pain of a million needles. Squeezing himself into his coat with a shiver, he hurried his steps.

The sidewalks were filled with people rushing to their homes or to the closest cafeteria to meet their friends and have a hot cup of coffee. The first Halloween decorations and sales had appeared in many of the shops' windows.

Kids on the streets laughed and yelled, running from one shop to the other, preparing for what was the most exciting night of the whole year, together with Christmas.

Dave wasn't even sure he ever liked Halloween. When he was a child, he used to go trick or tricking.

However, the only children who agreed to go with him were his brother and cousins, and it was because they had to, not because they enjoyed his company.

While he loved to read and draw, the others were all playing football or video games. Since elementary school, he was considered a weirdo.

Without a steady thought in his mind, he stopped in front of one of those windows and sighed. Those days when he went with his family to buy a costume for the party returned to his mind.

The day he chose to dress as a ghost came back to his memory. His lips curled upward, as that had been his best Halloween ever.

From under the blanket, his discomfort in being with other kids disappeared, and he was more social than he ever was.

That white screen was his protection from the outside world and made him braver, funnier, and happier.

Now, if it were possible to wear a mask in his everyday life, he might have had better chances to socialize and refine those skills.

Dave was a handsome guy in his mid-thirties, and in his life, he had only a few acquaintances and even fewer girlfriends.

Most of those were more friends who happened to be girls than real relationships; he was still a virgin and was sure he was destined to remain as such.

Dark blue eyes created a beautiful contrast with his raven hair, which framed a perfect oval face. To complete the picture was a slender body; he exercised daily, either by walking the whole distance from his home to his office or jogging whenever the weather allowed.

Physical exercise kept him from having long, idle moments where he would have watched TV, feeling sorry for himself, which was something he hated.

His residence was located on the second floor of a building at the border of the city. It wasn't a large one, just a two-room apartment he rented for a reasonable price.

The neighborhood wasn't one of the best, and often police had to come and intervene for cases of domestic violence, drugs, or prostitution.

Nights might have been noisy, but at least never dull, and with that in mind, Dave considered it the right contrast to balance his gray existence.

With a light jog, he rushed into the building. He hoped to get home as soon as possible, to have a long shower and a warm dinner to console his soul and satisfy his appetite.

As usual, he came in and looked around to make sure nobody had barged in and that everything was in order.

For him, it was a sort of ritual, although he knew that if a thief had intruded in his apartment, he would have been quite disappointed in finding nothing worth stealing.

Following a humble lifestyle, the only valuable item was his computer. That was the only thing he was willing to spend money on without coming to any compromise.

Drawing had been his passion since he was born. When he discovered digital art as a teenager, he used every penny to purchase new software to feed his creativity.

He wished to become a cartoonist for the newspaper, but that dream seemed too distant to even be conceived.

The only job he got was as an editor, so when he was at home, he entered his own world made of superheroes and comic art characters.

If he was supposed to be invisible in real life, then he decided to create a world where he was the hero and the star. There, he was appreciated and had friends, and also a girlfriend.

From outside his apartment, all sorts of muffled sounds came to his ears, but suddenly a noise he'd never heard before grabbed his attention.

It was like someone carried something weighty, either by dragging it or lifting and dropping it to the floor or the elevators.

With a slight groan, he stood up from the chair in front of his computer and remained for a moment to listen. He held his breath until it was clear enough that someone was relocating in or out. "I wonder who's the poor soul who had to move here."

Unable to keep the curiosity to himself, he walked to the door and left it ajar to peek from the little crack, hoping not to be spotted.

Someone was moving to the apartment at the end of the corridor. *That place has been empty for years. I bet the owner is more than glad to be able to either sell or to rent the property. As for the new tenant, I can only be sorry; he or she has no idea what kind of rat-hole this place is.*

The sound of footsteps brought him back from his consideration. The new tenant was coming from the stairs, bringing some heavy pieces of furniture or suitcase, so he stayed in the doorway to look at the new neighbor.

He was almost paralyzed when his glance met Her. In his whole life, he'd never seen such a beautiful girl.

Long red hair falling into soft curls upon her shoulders was the first thing he spotted. What enchanted him the most was the shiny coppery highlights like the sparkling of thousand stars.

She was petite and had a fabulous pair of legs showing from the miniskirt she was wearing, like something he'd seen only in fashion magazines.

As if caught in a spell, he remained to admire her, knowing an insignificant presence like his would have gone unnoticed by a graceful creature such as she.

"Fucking piece of shit!" she yelled as she stumbled on something as she came inside the apartment.

Well, perhaps she's a fallen angel – he considered, hearing her cursing.

Like the vision in a dream, she appeared to him coming from the door. With an elegant move, her head turned in the direction of Dave, and for a moment, their gazes met.

For the first time, someone was acknowledging his presence. But wanting to be sure, and not wanting to risk embarrassing himself, he kept the same position, waiting for someone from one of the other apartments to talk to her.

That didn't happen, and the awkward sensation of having given the worst impression of himself grabbed his soul. "Are you going to stare at me for the rest of the evening?" Her voice resounded through the corridor, as she placed her hands on her hips.

A beautiful, amused smile appeared on her face. Dave looked behind him, and when he didn't spot anyone, he realized she was talking to him. "Uh... I-I didn't mean..." A confused mumble came out of his mouth as his hands plunged into his pockets at the unexpected reaction. *Did she really see me?*

"Whatever you meant, I don't mind if you do, but as you do so, you could even help me out with the move. Here I am all alone!" she exclaimed, wondering about that strange guy almost trapped between the door of his flat.

"Oh ... but for sure ... just a second," he jolted as if he was waking up from a dream.

He flashed into his apartment to get his coat and keys to go and help the mysterious angel who was moving in.

"Thanks, my name is Gloria," she introduced herself with a smile as she saw Dave coming.

"Pleased to meet you, Gloria. I'm D-Dave," he mumbled with a nervous twitch on his lips, shaking her hand. Locking her eyes on his for an endless second, she gave him a vigorous handshake.

Her gaze pierced his soul like the stabbing of a knife, and as strange as it sounded, he was more than glad about it.

With a glance, she could touch the innermost part of his heart, and though many people would consider it rude, it was probably the best thing in his entire life.

The green color shining in her eyes was as bright as the grass after a thunderstorm, and she was wearing a lovely perfume, patchouli if he wasn't mistaken. He was enchanted by her.

"So, I don't have much to bring in, but the chests are all quite heavy. If we work together, we can solve it in a few minutes," Gloria's voice interrupted his thoughts.

"Of course." Dave walked to the stairs, following her to the van parked outside.

The trunk of the vehicle was still full of small packages and a couple of large chests, like those used back in the days when women got married. Those you would have found in your grandma's home, which contained all the linen brought as a dowry. In his opinion, it was uncommon for a girl like her to have this kind of furniture.

She immediately acknowledged the way he was looking at those chests and considered it extremely cute. "Those two belonged to my grandmother," she clarified. "When she passed away, I got them, as I was the only one interested in having them. My brothers weren't into those things and were ready to throw them away or to sell them at a thrift shop. I'm not a fan of these kinds of things either, but they're undeniably handy when it comes to moving away. Nothing is more resilient, and you can fit more things in it than in a standard box."

"You're not very talkative, are you?" she scrutinized him as they were carrying the first chest together.

"Honestly, I'm not used to talking to people," he admitted, instantly regretting his words. *Now she thinks I'm a freak!*

Instead, she laughed. "To whom do you talk then? To ghosts?"

A chuckle relieved his inner tension. "No... well, generally people don't even see me, so I spend quite a lonely existence. When you talked to me, I was taken by surprise. I was sure, like all the others, you couldn't see me."

They entered her apartment and left the chest in the living room, or whatever that room was supposed to be.

"Are you a sort of invisible man?" she joked, trying to comb her hair with her hands.

"I have no idea, but as strange as it might seem, people fail to notice my presence. Even at my job, I walk around, and nobody seems to acknowledge I've arrived. I can spend the whole day without exchanging a word with anyone," he answered with a miserable grin twisting his face.

"Perhaps you should start saying something to people," Gloria offered as they reached the van to get the second chest. "If you keep silent, you give the impression that you're the one who doesn't want to have any contact with them. It's an endless circle if you don't engage in a discussion. The rest of the world might think you want to keep your distance."

Dave thought for a moment about that possibility, and he admitted she wasn't wrong. "The problem is I don't know what to say," he protested, tilting his head as if to ask for help. "At my work, there are those columnists who are all fun and charm. I'll never be able to compete with them. Moreover, if I start to behave like them, other people might react, and I'm afraid they'll never like me."

"Well, you'll never know if you never try. Why don't you do the same as you did with me? Obviously, you're capable of having a conversation with people. What you need is a kick in your butt, like I did when I asked you to help me."

They carried the last chest into the room, and after a couple of other trips to the van, they brought in the rest of the boxes and suitcases. "Thanks for your help, Dave. I wish I could offer you a coffee, but as you can see, I barely have a bed here." She looked around, trying to decide where she should start unpacking.

"There's no need, and if you want, you can come to have coffee at my place. My apartment is not a royal palace, but I can still invite people in. You'll be the first who has visited my house, besides the electrician or the plumber," Dave proposed.

After a quick look around, she considered the offer for a second. "Well, why not? It's better to start knowing someone in the neighborhood, so perhaps you can tell me something about the people who live in this building.

Even an invisible man might know something about what's going on around here," Gloria giggled, closing the door behind her and following Dave.

Ceremoniously, he opened the door of his apartment. "Welcome to my humble abode," he invited her inside with a light bow.

At first glance, he hoped his place wasn't too messy to have guests. He was desperate to make a good impression.

With a swift move, he freed the couch of some clothes to allow her to sit down, then he walked to the kitchen to prepare the coffee.

That was the first time someone came for a visit. Besides the strange sensation of being in a weird situation, his soul was in a state of unrest.

He remembered the times when his mother had her friends coming for a chat, and he was always hiding in his bedroom.

It wasn't a question of disliking her friends, it was the certainty they would grab his cheeks, which at his age were full and rosy, something impossible for them to resist.

Moreover, they were all smoking, and the stench of their cigarettes was something he could not stand.

Gloria took a swift, visual tour of the apartment. "I have to admit you are quite brave to invite someone into your house whom you've never met before. I might be a criminal," she examined the pictures he had on the wall.

Bringing the two cups to the table, Dave smiled. "I might say the same about you. I could have asked you here intending to rape and kill you, and the coffee could be poisoned, for example."

"Touché," she averted her glance from his, taking her cup. "I'll take the risk. In my life, I've acquired a fair knowledge of human nature, and I doubt seriously you're the kind of person who would even think about being a serial killer."

"They're the most unsuspected people, so..." Dave pursued.

"Are you trying to scare or impress me?" An amused giggle escaped her.

"None of the two. I was putting things into perspective. This isn't a good neighborhood, and especially in this building, you won't have the time to get bored if you keep your eyes open," Dave started to explain. "Since I don't engage in social relationships, and most of the time, I'm invisible to them, I have lots of time to notice what is going on around me. It makes me feel less lonely."

Gloria wanted to know as much as possible about life in that building, and her curiosity was more than legitimate. *The first thing when moving to a new environment is to immediately get a clear idea about the neighbors and safety issues.*

Yet, Dave wasn't sure whether she should have asked those questions to the police since they were regularly visiting the building.

"Do you mean things might get dangerous?" she wondered, biting her lower lip.

"I can't say anything about the danger level for a woman. Take, for example, the family at the opposite end of the corridor from your apartment. There's often a fight going on between the man, who I guess is an alcoholic, and the wife," he pointed his finger in its direction. "They can be vociferous, and when the guy who is living beside them is getting pissed enough, the whole building knows about it."

Taking a short pause to consider what to say, he leaned on the couch. "Upstairs, I wouldn't dare to go; at least once a month the police are visiting, and they're bringing someone with them.

"There aren't any loud noises coming out of there, but I suspect they're dealing drugs. It's better if you avoid the road on the other side of the flat house, where there is the parking lot; from there, gunshots can be heard, so if you have a car, you should park it somewhere else."

"Nice neighborhood indeed," Gloria smirked. "I'll try to be careful."

"Not to sound offensive, but I suggest you dress... more. There are people here who don't have any trouble with raping girls, and this is something which happens quite often." Dave started to talk in a lower tone of voice, like he didn't even want her to hear what he was saying.

He was afraid she would think it was his opinion that a girl is raped because of her way of dressing. "Please, don't get me wrong. I don't mean at all to say it's the fault of the girl's clothing if she gets assaulted. What I want to say is, with a pair of jeans, there is more time for someone to intervene and help you..." Averting his glance from her, he entwined his fingers and twisted them.

"It has happened often?" Gloria nodded calmly, understanding what he meant.

"Unfortunately, yes. I could stop an assault a couple of times because the rapist took more time to..." he breathed, lowering his gaze.

"I'll try my best to keep myself safe, thank you." She held his hand gently.

They remained silent for a moment, sipping their coffee. "So, what do you do?" she asked, breaking the ice.

"As I said, I work at the local newspaper, nothing fancy on that. For the rest, I just survive, and try to cope with the failures in my life." His voice flickered.

She sighed. "Well, I think I need to go back home and start unpacking things. The apartment is basically furnished but there is no mattress on the bed, which won't arrive until tomorrow. I'm also thinking about whether it might be best to search for a hotel, as I don't have a bed in my place. Do you know any decent place around here?"

"No, I don't know, but if you want, you can use my computer to find something. Although, I might suggest searching in a better area. You might call a taxi and ask him to bring you to some hotel," he suggested.

"That's a great idea. There's a cab stand not far from here," Gloria considered, standing up. "Thanks for the help, and see you around."

Already feeling alone and missing her presence, he walked her to the door. "Yes, sure, sleep well, and good luck with everything. I hope we will meet again," he murmured as he watched her walking away.

Be careful, Gloria, this place is more dangerous than you can ever believe, Dave thought as he closed the door. He went to sit on the couch, where a minute before, he was entertaining a conversation with her.

Her perfume lingered in the air, and he indulged in the fragrance as if to feel her presence.

***

From that day on, it was challenging to see Gloria, either in the corridor or anywhere else.

Fearing she would think he was trying to intrude in her life, he didn't dare to come to ring her bell.

He hoped to meet her again, having the chance to talk to her, but this didn't happen. At a certain point, he feared she had moved away, being scared by the neighborhood or the people hanging around there.

His life returned to the usual routine, and he almost forgot about her, until one day things started to change.

He wondered how he couldn't have seen this before. Maybe because it began gradually and I didn't have the time to spot anything of what was going on, and perhaps Gloria could see me because, like me, she's invisible.

It was definitely not the first one he had noticed, and her visitors were coming after sunset.

Dave was returning from work one evening when he saw her greeting a man at the door.

She wasn't properly 'dressed,' and they exchanged a fast glance before he hurried back to his apartment. "We're all miserable souls here in this part of the city. You knew where you were going to live when you rented the apartment, and it was the reason why you chose to come here," he muttered to himself.

Shaking his head, he prepared a coffee for himself. He looked around at the place where he was living. "This place needs to be put in order. I have let myself go recently and, looking around, this isn't the place I would like to invite anyone, not even the plumber, for that matter," he said.

Starting from the kitchen, he emptied all the counters to clean thoroughly and reorganize them.

Since it was Friday, he didn't have any specific time for going to sleep, and with that in mind, he went through the whole apartment until it was spotless.

It took him until one o'clock in the morning when he'd collected a big bag of trash full of things he didn't need and forgot about.

Probably, it wasn't the right time to go out and throw the garbage away. The streets became dangerous right after sunset.

Nevertheless, he couldn't leave the bags to rot until the day after. At least, not now that the apartment was spotless, for once.

With a deep breath, he walked outside to the bins along the street.

The night was calm, and the neighborhood was strangely silent. Not a noise could be heard, and it appeared as if everybody was sleeping.

I guess even the bad guys need to sleep from time to time, he considered, looking around. As he was returning inside the building, he stumbled into a strange guy.

It came to his mind: Humphrey Bogart in Casablanca, as the man seemed to be coming out from an old detective movie.

The man, wearing a fedora hat and a dark raincoat, offered Dave a fast glance. Without even saying a word, not even apologizing or asking for apologies, he rushed away, disappearing in the light mist rising during the evening hours.

Open-mouthed, Dave stood frozen, watching him in awe as he disappeared through the fog.

The first question crossing his mind was what a person like him was doing in a place like that, when he recalled he could have been one of Gloria's late-night visitors.

Climbing the last flight of stairs to reach his corridor, he hesitated, staring toward the closed door of her apartment.

A couple of long moments passed by as his mind formulated too many questions to which there wouldn't be an easy answer. In particular, he wondered if it was the right time for him to knock at her door, asking whether everything was fine.

As if to cast the thought away, he shook his head. Perhaps it was better to forget about her.

She was one of the many faces in that tall, gray building, one of the many stories, and one day she would disappear without leaving a trace.

With a whimper, he opened the door of his apartment and was almost surprised to see it looking like he'd never seen before.

Everything was in order, clean, and ready for receiving guests. The only problem was that there wouldn't be any guest in his house, as it was a place meant only to soothe his own miseries.

From under the sheets of his bed he stared at the ceiling, without the chance to find any sleep. All the thoughts that swirled in his mind kept him more awake than during the day.

The silence, almost unnatural, which seemed to blanket the whole world, was something he wasn't used to. Everything was too quiet.

He feared something would happen soon enough, and it would be something terrible. "I wonder why in this world I have to think about some disaster. Perhaps people need to sleep, and maybe the world is turning to become a better place even in a rat-hole like this one," he spelled aloud.

Closing his eyes, he finally fell slowly asleep.

CHAPTER 2

'A sense of grogginess completed by foggy memories of the previous night welcomed Dave to a new day.

Sitting up in the bed required an effort he'd never needed before. Glancing around from his seated position, it was clear that standing up might be even more challenging.

A loud groan escaped his mouth as he stood on his feet and walked toward the window. He opened the blinds, and with a grimace twisting his face, he acknowledged another gray day.

On a positive note, the rain wasn't falling anymore, and a shy sun filtered through the thin curtain of clouds, which at least allowed him to go for a jog to the park.

Thinking about having free time on the weekends made him wonder about the meaning these two days held for different people.

For most of them, Saturday and Sunday weren't just days when they could rest and forget about the job, but also a chance to spend some time with friends and family. "And this is what I would do, too, if I had any. My only friend is Gloria, but I doubt she's in the mood for socializing. I guess she socialized enough during the week, and besides, I'm not sure whether she even thinks about having a break. After all, general customers tend to use these two days for this sort of thing," he went to prepare his first cup of coffee.

Again, he marveled at the cleanliness and order in his house and decided this would be the way he would keep it every day. "Once I made an effort to clean as deeply as I did last night, it shouldn't require much to maintain the same conditions." The heavenly aroma of the coffee wafted from the coffee maker.

He switched on the TV to listen to the newscast. "Always bad news," he growled, as he unceremoniously placed the dirty dishes in the dishwasher. "I wonder why they never give space to positivity; people would be in a better mood knowing something good is happening besides the usual. This way, it seems like the world is going literally to pieces."

Slowly shaking his head, he prepared to go for a jog, taking advantage of the dry weather.

One more time, before climbing down the stairs, he turned to give a swift glance to Gloria's door.

Walking the streets, he spotted the same man he stumbled into the previous night. Dave followed him with his eyes and realized he walked in the direction of his building.

He should mind his own business, but curiosity won over reason and rationality. Therefore, he decided to follow him to understand whether he was one of Gloria's visitors, or if he had another destination.

Trying to keep a safe distance, he followed the mysterious Humphrey Bogart. With a muffled chuckle, he considered calling him that from that moment on. He tailed him walking inside the building, and from his position, he watched him taking the stairs to reach the second floor.

He peeked from the corner of the staircase to follow his moves.

The man glanced stealthily around to make sure he was alone, and only then, he knocked at Gloria's apartment. Dave didn't expect him to knock at the door. Like all the other apartments, it had a doorbell.

Nevertheless, it seemed like he used a sort of code, three fast knocks close to each other – pause – one single knock – pause – and other two quick knocks.

It appeared to be something they both agreed to. When she opened, wearing only dark green lace lingerie, Dave took the chance offered by his position to get a glimpse of her beauty. *I've never seen anything so graceful*, he thought, retreating as soon as Humphrey Bogart entered the apartment.

As the door closed behind the man, Dave couldn't hold his curiosity any longer and tiptoed toward the entrance of Gloria's apartment. *What the hell am I doing?* He reproached himself. *Think, if someone comes out of an apartment and sees you eavesdropping at her door!* With that thought, he walked away as quickly and as silently as possible, resuming his jog to the park.

Following the man who reached her door as he came in was already something he regretted.

Even though whatever happened in her house was none of his business, curiosity overwhelmed his common sense.

Gloria wasn't only the most beautiful woman he'd ever talked to. She also was the only one who could apparently see him – the first one who spoke to him, making her dear to Dave's heart.

It didn't matter whether the whole neighborhood judged her harshly for the job she'd chosen for herself.

He knew the hardships of making a living in their society and didn't have any reason to judge her choice. They were quite similar to each other – they were both invisible.

As he thought about it, a tear tickled along his cheek. The bitterness for the misery he simply accepted as something intended for him, rose from the innermost part of his soul.

Just like some people are destined to be successful, others are meant to be nothing at all. That conviction was no longer sufficient. He wanted more; he wanted the impossible: Gloria only for himself.

Trying desperately to stop thinking about her and fighting against his arousal, he ran as fast as his body allowed. He hoped the physical strain would help him to think clearly, but that didn't happen.

Panting and drenched in sweat, he collapsed on the closest bench, trying to regain some breath. "Stop thinking about her," he reproached himself. "Can't you be happy with the fact that she had spoken to you, and she can see you?"

Dave remained for a moment pondering the question he just formulated and stood from the bench. "No, I can't..."

Before he decided to return home, he continued to jog for another hour. As he approached his apartment building, he spotted a police car.

This didn't concern him particularly; it was almost normal to have them coming on weekends when perhaps people started to drink a bit more.

What instead attracted his attention was the number of people who left their apartments and grouped outside.

"What's going on?" he asked, reaching the first bystander waiting with the rest of the crowd.

"I don't know; I don't live here, but according to what I heard, a man was murdered last night, and this morning someone found his corpse in front of his apartment at the top floor." He barely looked at him, keeping his eyes to what happened in the building.

"Well, this isn't the first time. I wonder why people were evacuated from the place," Dave grumbled to himself.

"The suspect for the murder has taken one of the tenants as a hostage," a young lady intervened to explain what took place in the last two hours.

With his heart jumping in his chest, Dave glanced around in the desperate attempt to find Gloria. He wanted to be reassured she wasn't the one who had been held in the hands of a maniac who probably would hurt her.

As his gaze toured the surroundings in vain, his breath choked in his throat. With his legs hardly holding him upright, he struggled toward the apartment building, hoping to talk to one of the officers.

"You cannot enter," an officer warned, placing himself in front of him. His heart raced in his chest, and his hands were shaking as he turned to look at the entrance, holding his emotions to keep his mind clear.

"I... Who is the person kidnapped?"

"We don't have his identity yet, but we're making sure the whole building has been evacuated. Do you have any idea about who the hostage might be?" The officer scrutinized Dave through narrowed eyelids.

"I hope I'm wrong, but a girl is living down the hall from me, and I don't see her here outside. Of course, she might also be somewhere else, and maybe nothing's happened to her, but... She lives on the second floor." His breath was short, and his hands started to become damp with sweat. "Who is inside? Did you establish any contact with the kidnapper?"

"Sir, I understand you're worried about your friend, but the best you can do is to wait here, together with all the others, while we attempt to get in touch with him. In the meantime, you can stop by the police van. You might want to give them all the information about this girl, just in case she's the one who has been kidnapped, but at the moment there is nothing else you can do."

Dave averted his glance toward the vehicle.

His heart raced faster and faster, making it almost impossible for him to breathe as he walked in its direction, hoping to obtain better information. "Excuse me, but perhaps I know the person who has been held hostage," he commenced, approaching one of the two officers coordinating the operation.

One of them suddenly turned his gaze and scrutinize Dave from head to feet. "How can you know who is?"

"Well, I didn't say I do for sure, but I have a suspicion about who she might be, and I hope I'm wrong." He hesitated, confused, lowering his gaze.

"Then you should go back with the others and wait until we resolve this situation. Please be assured it won't take long, and soon you'll all be free to return to your homes," the police officer replied.

"I have my doubts about your confidence." Dave turned to face the apartment building, praying for Gloria or whoever the hostage was, to come out.

"This is my job." He toughened his expression, brows tightening together. "Now, please, go back and don't interfere. The more you keep us busy with your questions, the more difficult it will be to get your friend out of there."

Dave sighed. The whole situation didn't make any sense. Still, he followed the officer's advice and joined the same group of people who were waiting outside, hoping to find some answers.

He spotted a woman who lived with her family on the third floor, sobbing loudly and yelling confused words in her despair.

He hardly recognized her from the happy-looking woman he used to know. Through her tears, she barely acknowledged his presence there.

After all, he was still an insignificant, invisible creature in the world, and possibly the woman wasn't keen on talking with a stranger.

"What's going on?" Frustration began to grab his heart, as apparently nobody really knew what happened.

She raised her glance to him as if she wondered where the voice came from.

"Johnny, her son, is the guy who is keeping a hostage," explained a man who held her, caressing her shoulders to soothe her.

"I can't believe it. Why would he do something like that?" Dave wondered.

The woman wriggled from the arms of the man. "Early this morning, he left the house telling me he intended to meet Spike, one of his friends. I never liked him; he's always in trouble with the law. I warned my Johnny not to hang out with him, or he would have the same troubles as him," the woman went on, sobbing and gesticulating.

"Spike is the victim?" Dave asked, remaining open-mouthed, unable to believe what he heard.

"Yes, and God only knows he deserved to die, but my son didn't kill him. I'm afraid he panicked and feared he would go to jail, accused of murder." She collapsed in the arms of the man who seemed very close to her and the boy.

With a slight nod, Dave continued, "I also believe he wasn't the murderer. Have you already talked to the police? Or can you talk to your son on his phone?"

The woman tilted her head, scanning him with questioning eyes. "Where the hell did you come from? Do you think they will listen to me? Since when do they listen to black people?

They can't wait to slam my boy in jail for a crime he never committed." Her voice was bitter and defeated at the possibility that a sentence was already pronounced.

Dave shook his head. "Come with me. We need to tell this to the officers, and you have to contact him. Johnny probably thinks he's accused of murder. If nobody reassures him by telling him he's not, he might do something stupid."

With those words, Dave collected all the strength he had in his body. Fighting against his shyness, fearing what could happen to Gloria, he grabbed Johnny's mother's hand, pulling her away from the man and walked her to the police officer.

He didn't know Johnny well enough to say they were friends, but an invisible man has more time to observe people, and he knows them better than anyone else.

"Where are you bringing me? Let me go!" she protested, wriggling from his hold.

Dave turned to look into her eyes. "Do you want to have a chance to save him, or would you prefer to have him accused of something he didn't do?"

"Of course, I want to help him, but they won't listen to me, and by the way, who are you?"

"I live on the second floor. I can't say I know Johnny, but I have been living here long enough to tell who is who, and your son is not a murderer," he attempted to explain, maintaining his calm.

"But I've never seen you around." She looked at him through narrowed eyes.

"Nobody does..." Whining, he resumed his walk with the woman to the police van.

It took less than another hour to resolve the situation and having Johnny coming out of the apartment. The officers brought him to the department for an interrogation.

Since there wasn't any proof connecting him to the murder, he was released with a warning for having taken Gloria as a hostage.

Even that was an overstatement, Dave thought, listening to the rumors, which continued to be discussed in the following week.

Johnny was simply hiding in her apartment, hoping to escape the police. He was more scared than her when he barged in.

The investigation over the death of Spike went on for half a year. Apparently, the killer disappeared like the shadows of the night.

Nevertheless, this unsolved crime left all the inhabitants of the building shaken. It wasn't because of the assassination perpetrated under their noses, which was something they were sadly used to.

Deep inside, everybody hoped someone would kill Spike, and besides, his lifestyle suggested a sudden and premature death.

Yet, nobody ever dared to admit how glad they were for his murder. He used to deal with drugs and had been in jail for domestic violence against his girlfriend, who was brought safely away from him.

He was also considered responsible for the rape of another teenage girl who lived in the same building.

The girl never wanted to reveal the identity of the rapist because she feared him. Still, everybody seemed to know it had been Spike.

Indeed, he wasn't the only rotten apple living in the area, and there were worse individuals than him.

Spike got judged more harshly because he'd brought a good boy like Johnny down the wrong path. The boy was only seventeen years old, and since the father had left the family, he tried to find a father figure outside of his home.

Spike offered him, in a sort of sick way, an alternative, making him feel accepted by someone who was considered an authority by the rotten part of society.

He had women, money, and power. Everybody was scared of him and being welcomed as one of his team members was, for Johnny, a way to become a man.

If you cannot take the boy far from the bad guys, then you need to eliminate them, Dave thought as he left his apartment to reach his work. He wasn't afraid to admit he was glad about Spike's murder.

Still, he also understood his death didn't solve the criminality problem in the neighborhood.

Someone has to take more time to raise those kids and give them a better alternative than the criminal life. Perhaps if those boys could see what's going to happen to criminals, they might think twice before joining their lifestyle. He wasn't sure he really believed it, but certainly, the attraction to power could overwhelm the younger generations. *Well, how can I blame them? After all, if I give them my example, they would all run to the first criminal to become like them, rather than like me, an invisible man.*

Entering the building of the newspaper where he worked, he visually toured the environment.

People walked around and didn't acknowledge he came inside.

With a light sigh, he sauntered to his office, ready for another day. "Well, at least I can keep my job," he considered closing the door of his room behind him. "If I had to search for employment, I would stay unemployed forever with my invisibility."

Sitting in front of his computer, he started to work, trying to forget about his personal problems and focus on his daily duties until he returned home.

His mind was still attempting to divert his attention toward Gloria, the death of Spike, and Johnny, and for the rest of the day, he couldn't concentrate on his task.

A nagging voice in the back of his head reproached him for not going to visit Gloria and asking whether she needed any help after the incident. "Even though Johnny was more scared than her, it must have been a shock for Gloria having a stranger intruding in her apartment."

His voice whispering as he stretched his back on the chair, surprised him.

Every time he stepped in front of her door, the desire to ring her bell seemed overwhelming, but the fear of rejection forced him to give up.

She's always busy with the mysterious Humphrey Bogart, who appeared to be a steady customer for her. I'm not surprised; despite being a prostitute, she's a charming girl, he thought.

Dave glanced at the clock. Time seemed to have stopped, and there was no way to make it run again.

He had many things to do, and he needed to do them all by the end of the morning, to focus on the next articles to be edited.

The strict timetables didn't give any mercy, and it was impossible to break them or ask for more time to have them done.

Considering seeking help in a cup of coffee, he stood, hoping a bit of caffeine would help him to concentrate on his duties, rather than on his personal life.

A couple of journalists gathered to talk in front of their first coffee, and as usual, nobody saw Dave coming in. They barely acknowledged him when he walked by them to get a mug and reach the machine.

They were busy talking and chattering and couldn't be bothered by an invisible presence like him.

The thought that they didn't know an editor was checking up on their articles, or whether they knew who he was, amused his mind.

Shaking his head, considering his question completely irrelevant, he turned away to leave the kitchen. As he reached the door, Joseph stormed in, and they stumbled against each other, causing the coffee in Dave's mug to spill on his shirt.

"Fuck!" he muttered.

"Watch where you're walking!" Joseph growled, annoyed as the others giggled at the incident.

Surprised at his comment, Dave lifted his eyes to glance at him, hoping to have at least an apology, but he already started talking with a couple of reporters and continued ignoring him.

Dave huffed, disappointed, walked to the coffee machine, and refilled his mug.

He left the room and headed to the restroom to clean his shirt. It wasn't something that would have solved anything, but the stain was less visible afterward.

The only solution would have been to have a spare to change into if accidents like this keep happening.

The incident would probably not repeat itself, but I would be safe from any further embarrassment, he considered as he tried to remove the coffee spot.

He observed his image in the mirror. "Joseph barely saw me. I wonder what sort of magic I'm cursed with if nobody can even see me, except for people who, like me, are invisible."

Staring in the mirror, he almost expected his reflection to fade away.

Nevertheless, no matter how long and carefully he kept his eyes on his reflection, nothing happened, and he was like everybody else.

He had a physical body, indeed. Yet, nobody seemed to see him. Dave shook his head and decided to get over the incident.

After all, his invisibility wasn't something new. He'd carried it with him since he was born, so there should have been nothing surprising about it.

He returned to his office and tried all he could to forget about all the other issues. Now, he needed to concentrate on his job, or he would be late, causing an embarrassing delay for the whole newspaper.

At that point, he would no longer be invisible. Still, between invisibility and being blamed, he evidently preferred the first option.

Days went by, and soon enough, the life in the building where he lived returned to roll in the same old way.

Spike's death was nothing more than a memory; one of the many casualties that happen when you decide to live your life on the other side of legality.

Police couldn't find any suspect. Whoever the killer was, he intruded inside the house, killing Spike, leaving no trace of DNA or anything to lead to anybody living in the world. Initially, there were some rumors of something supernatural which killed Spike, but eventually, this option was soon discarded.

As life went by, other troubles filled up the minds of the inhabitants of the neighborhood, bringing insignificance to that particular crime.

One thing Dave noticed was that since the murder of Spike, the mysterious Humphrey Bogart never showed up again to visit Gloria. "I'm wondering why. Some might say he was involved in the murder, but this is something I seriously doubt," he whispered as he climbed the stairs to reach the second floor.

Still immersed in his thoughts, he found himself in front of Gloria's apartment. Perhaps it was time for him to pay a visit to her, hoping she was not busy with her customers.

Without even thinking twice, he rang the bell, and already as he waited, he regretted the choice.

He was almost ready to leave when she appeared at the door in her lace underwear. Dave blushed to unbelievable colors and didn't have anything to say in front of her beauty.

"Well, look who is here." A bright, surprised smile flashed on her face. "Do you want to come in, or you prefer to remain there?"

"May I come in?" He gingerly placed the first step into the house.

"Of course," she allowed him to enter the apartment and closing the door behind him. "So, to what do I owe the pleasure? Are you here for business or for something else?" she joked.

Dave didn't know what to say. He had to admit Gloria was his best chance to, at least, lose his virginity, but he wasn't interested in sex without love.

Even though he had deeper feelings toward her, this wasn't enough, knowing that it would have been nothing but cold, emotionless business for her. "I came here to see how you were doing. I wanted to come here earlier, but I was afraid you didn't want to talk to me. Besides, you've been quite busy, without any particular working schedule, so I wasn't sure when would be a good time to visit," he tried to justify himself.

She went to put on a pink satin dressing gown. "I thought you didn't want to have anything to do with me because of my job. Many people keep a distance from those like me."

"No, I don't mind what you do for a living. That is none of my business. I even wanted to ask you out for another coffee, but I never had the guts to come here. When I came back from my jog to find out you'd been held hostage, I thought my heart was going to explode. I don't believe he had any intentions of hurting you, but in a desperate situation, people don't act rationally anymore." He twisted his fingers to overcome the embarrassment of opening his soul.

"That kid was more frightened than anyone else. He came into this apartment, intruding from the window in the restroom. When he saw me coming, he was completely terrified," Gloria recalled, taking a seat on the couch where Dave was also seated. "He mumbled it wasn't him who killed Spike and didn't want to go to jail for something he didn't do. I tried to make him understand that, in this way, he made things more difficult, as the police had already arrived. It wasn't easy to calm him down, and obviously, the kid wouldn't be able to harm a fly."

"His mother was in a panic when I returned from jogging..." Suddenly, Dave's mind went blank.

He lowered his gaze to his feet, trying to find something to say. Due to his invisibility problem, his life hadn't been very social.

Those communication skills that distinguish people like Joseph and other people from his work hadn't had the chance to develop for himself.

His eyes were drawn now and then to Gloria's body peeking through the dressing gown, and he was ashamed for feeling aroused.

Gloria understood and felt sorry for his embarrassment. She was sure if she had been dressed differently, Dave wouldn't feel so uncomfortable.

She suspected he had a soft spot for her, differently than all her customers. He liked her in a way nobody else did.

Trying to focus his attention on something else besides her body, Dave looked around at the place.

"You have a nice-looking place here," he said matter-of-factly.

Gloria giggled. "Thank you. Would you like a coffee? I owe you one."

"Why not? Thanks." He glanced around the apartment.

That was the first time he'd been inside since the time he'd helped her move her luggage.

"I have a better idea. I'm not expecting any customers until later tonight. Why don't we go out? You will be less embarrassed if we're in neutral territory and if I wear something more than this dressing gown," she proposed.

"That's a great idea," his voice chirped with enthusiasm. "I don't mean to say I don't like the way you look... I think you're beautiful... I just think..."

"Don't you worry, I understand perfectly. Also, for me, it would be better if I don't mix personal life with business." She winked.

Dave feared he was falling in love with her if it wasn't so that he loved her since the first moment he set eyes on her.

Without another word, she went to her bedroom and changed her clothes. After a few minutes, she reappeared wearing a pair of jeans and a black shirt. "Are we ready?" she asked, grabbing her jacket and slipping into her shoes.

With a broad smile, Dave stood from the couch. "Sure, let's go!"

They walked the streets for a while, without exchanging any words. Despite the many times he wanted to go and ring her bell to talk with her or to make sure everything was fine, in that exact moment, he realized he had nothing enthralling to say.

Everything coming to his mind sounded quite meaningless. Keeping silent, they entered the cafeteria and took a seat close to the window.

"So, how is your work going?" Her voice brought him back to reality, breaking the imperceptible veil of silence building slowly between them.

"Oh... Well, nothing new happened. I spend my days in my office, and there isn't anything else for me to do but carry out my editing job." His voice returned to its relaxed tone, grateful for her understanding and patience.

He recalled the incident with Joseph and decided to discharge his frustration by telling her about it. "However, recently, I went to the kitchen to get my morning coffee. As I came out of the door, Joseph arrived like a freight train, and I poured the entire contents of the mug on my shirt." A bitter grin appeared on his face.

He held the menu in his hands as if to hold on the last hope, recalling the feeling of being ignored. "I decided to have a spare one to keep in my office if this sort of accident happens again. It was quite embarrassing to walk around with such a visible stain. I tried to wipe it away, but nothing helped."

"Hi, guys, what can I bring you?" The cheery voice of the waitress interrupted his bitterness. They both rushed to check the menu, trying to decide as quickly as possible.

"I'm going to have an espresso, please," Gloria stated, turning the list on the table.

"A hot chocolate for me, please." He just ordered the first drink that fell under his gaze.

The girl took their orders and left, trotting away happily.

Glancing back at Gloria, he tried to resume his story. "I have no idea why, but just like with Joseph, nobody notices me. Of course, if I had spilled coffee on his shirt, it would have been different. Instead, he simply growled, *'watch where you walk'* and continued to ignore me, talking with the other people who were gathered for a break."

"That was quite impolite of him; at least he could have apologized," Gloria snapped with an outraged tone in her voice.

"Who? Joseph?" With a tilt of his head, he glanced at the ceiling. "He never apologizes, as it's always someone else's fault."

"What a jerk!"

"There's nothing to do. It's the way he is," he shrugged.

"You shouldn't make excuses for him. If someone is rude toward you, then you should stop sheepishly withstanding his behavior." She pointed a finger against him as she spoke in a reproaching tone.

A low-pitched whimper escaped his mouth. "You're right, but if a nobody like me did anything similar and put him in his place, it would attract the wrath of the whole company. They all love him; he's one of the most skilled reporters, and besides, he has amazing social skills. He can charm everyone." He hoped that was enough to justify his spineless behavior.

Gloria grimaced, bending her head to a side. "How sad. I can feel the challenges of working in such an environment."

"Indeed, but since I have my own office and don't share projects with anyone else, I can survive until my retirement," Dave explained.

"That is quite far from now. You should think about your present, rather than the future. If you don't learn to stand your ground, then there will always be a bully who will take advantage of your good heart," Gloria replied.

"One day, I'll get even..." Dave smirked. "So, what about you? I think I told you the story of my life, but I know almost nothing about you. What I know is you have an unconventional job and are an adorable person. I would love to be your friend, in which case, we should get to know each other."

She sighed as the waitress returned with their orders. "You're right, but there isn't much of anything to say about me. I believe I'm one of the invisible people who populate this city. We're all the background music necessary to the orchestra. The audience won't acknowledge every instrument playing, but without some of them, the melody won't make any sense."

Dave smiled. "Why did you choose to be... well...? Was it even a choice?"

"It must sound strange enough, but yes, it was. Although it has been quite a while since the last time I met my family, my past isn't troubled. I can conduct my business in my apartment, and this allows me to select my clients and set my price.

"There isn't a ruthless monster forcing me to prostitute, and I don't search for my customers on the streets. They're my best marketers.

"They spread the word about my business to their friends, so I can be sure any guy who asks for an appointment will be a trusted one. Nevertheless, I do my own research before accepting a request from an unknown person," she started to explain. "The reason why I do this work is... well, why not? With what I earn, I can save money. In this way, I can count on good savings for the day I eventually retire. Then I'll move to some nice and cheap place and enjoy my golden years."

Dave stared, surprised at her confession. He'd always believed a person, whether woman or man, would have never chosen that path voluntarily.

Obviously, you will find differences between those girls who are forced to sell themselves on the streets and those who had a home where they could set up appointments with their clients. "I must admit this is the first time I considered prostitution under this point of view," Dave admitted, confused.

"It's a bit like in the porn business. Some actors are victims of low-quality scammers who produce nothing but junk. Others find quality producers who offer better standards to the customers and employees. Prostitution is quite similar to the porn industry; either you work on your own or become a victim of ruthless monsters. The choice isn't necessarily open..."

"I would have never suspected..." Dave mumbled.

CHAPTER 3

Days and months went by, and on a gray, foggy spring Saturday morning, Dave woke up from a nightmare he couldn't even remember.

A few confused images returned to his memory. Yet, nothing gave him the certainty it had to do with Gloria, the mysterious Humphrey Bogart, who never showed up again, or with Spike's death.

The blue lights of police cars filtered through the blinds, flashed rhythmically against the walls of the room.

Stretching his body, he stood from the bed and went to look at what had happened.

He didn't have a clear vision from his position and tried to lean a bit, spotting a couple of cop cars and some people outside looking around and chattering.

The scene in front of his eyes reminded him of the day when Spike got murdered. "Who was killed this time? Was it because of a fight between gangs or an accident?" Dave wondered to himself, trying to obtain a better visual of the street.

Without wasting any further time, he hurried to dress and rushed outside, curious to understand the reason for the police's presence.

He spotted a few bystanders, and he strode confidently toward them rather than disturbing the officers doing their job. "What's going on?" he asked casually as he approached a small group of people chattering together.

"Hard to say; I walked by when I saw those people in front of the building and the cop cars. According to what I've overheard, someone was killed last night, but I don't know the victim's identity," the man admitted.

"Does anyone know what's going on, besides the officers?" his voice rose a bit louder, turning around to gather everybody's attention.

A woman who was there, listening, intervened. "I live here, and early this morning, I was startled by loud noises coming from one of the apartments on my same floor. The first thing I thought to do was call the police to make them quiet, but when I was waiting for them to arrive, I heard gunshots. I was afraid that things would escalate, so I decided to wait outside."

"When did the shooting happen? Not a sound reached my apartment." Failing to understand how it was possible, Dave bit his lower lip, hoping for an explanation to come from them.

"Before sunrise. I can't say the exact time. Maybe from the other building, the shots sounded muffled, but here it seemed like we were at war. Then like a door had been slammed shut, everything went silent, and I thought one of the two groups died," she added. "As soon as I saw the police coming, I directed them to the apartment where I thought the noises came from."

"Do you think one of them got killed?" Dave wondered.

"I can't say, and to be honest, I don't even care. Those people are only troublemakers, to say the least. If the cops cannot, or won't help, we can only hope they will kill each other," she replied bitterly.

Furrowing his brows, he squeezed in his shoulders, abhorring such a way of thinking, but she was right.

Police arrived only after the crime – when a girl had been raped, or people got robbed or killed.

Not everybody living in the neighborhood was criminal, but those who were could terrorize them all.

The impression of being left alone to their destiny crept into the heart of the small community; everybody wished to witness the triumph of justice.

People were waiting for some explicit action from the government or the municipality to improve their quality of life. Their pleas remained unheard.

Silently, looking at his surroundings, he hoped for some news to come from the officers who were gathering information from those who lived in the building and collecting evidence on the crime scene.

As soon as he saw an officer who could answer his questions, Dave paced toward him. "Excuse me, Sir, can I ask you something?"

"Do you live here?" he asked.

"Well, not exactly here, but in his same complex." Dave pointed at the building on the other side of the road. "What has happened?"

"It seems like it was a fight between two gangs, but you will read about it in the newspapers," he cut him short.

Gathering every bit of his non-existent self-confidence, he resumed his quest for information. "Can't you tell me anything more about it?"

Crossing his arms across his chest, the officer took a small pause, just enough time to observe the man in front of him. "Are you a journalist?"

"Well... no, I'm just employed at the local newspaper." His voice trembled in hesitation, unwilling to reveal too much about his profession.

"Then you will hear about it when you go to work tomorrow," the officer walked away, leaving Dave with thousands of questions to which no other might answer.

He shook his head and decided to ask those people who were living on the same floor; perhaps they knew better and were more willing to share their knowledge with him.

"Where do you think you're going?" the officer asked, surprised when he noticed him walking to the entrance.

"Well, people are still inside, and if you don't mind, I'm going to check how they're doing," Dave was determined to enter no matter what.

"You can't yet come in; our forensics aren't done, and we asked the people of the whole building not to leave their apartments until we're ready. This means that if they cannot go outside, nobody else can come inside," the officer explained.

Dave lowered his head, defeated. Certainly, it was crucial to keep the crime scene free to avoid compromising the evidence.

With a whimper, he left, determined to watch the development of the situation from his window.

The only chance he had was to wait for the police to leave to go and ask around.

The other tenants could tell more than the officers could ever guess. Probably someone who might have seen something, even the killer, was willing to disclose the facts to him.

People might want to take justice into their own hands if law enforcement isn't more present around here, Dave thought.

Perhaps this is what they hope, that we will all kill each other so the problem will be solved. Shaking his head, he returned home.

As usual, reaching his floor, he glanced at the door of Gloria's place. He considered going to chat with her. *Maybe she heard something, and she was awake at that time.*

As he found himself at her door, he hesitated, wondering whether she'd been too busy to pay attention to what was going on outside her apartment.

Moreover, she might still be sleeping at this time of the morning. Biting his lower lip, he decided to wait until the early afternoon.

Within a couple of hours, though, the news of what had happened the previous night started to spread around.

Hearing someone from the corridor speaking rather heatedly about something made him extremely curious. Failing to understand what they were talking about, he guessed it was about the shooting in the other building.

Gingerly tiptoeing to the door, he wanted to go out to ask some questions. Nevertheless, he remained there to listen through the door to make sure they were arguing about it.

He opened the door as if he intended to go outside. "Sorry to interrupt you." His voice was almost a trembling whisper. "Are you talking about what happened last night?" Dave chimed in, expecting an adverse reaction from the two guys.

They both turned their gazes at him, considering him from head to toe, with a puzzled expression.

"What the hell do you want?" the voice of one of them thundered, echoing through the corridor.

"Hmm... I-I'm sorry to intrude on your discussion. I wondered if you have any news about what happened in the other building," Dave whimpered, embarrassed for his intrusion into a debate he'd never been invited to.

Their expressions relaxed, understanding they all wanted to get a clearer picture of the crimes perpetrated against the member of the local criminality.

"We overheard someone talking about a man dressed in a black coat who was spotted last night around here. We can't say whether it's true or a rumor," the other guy, who was more reasonable, explained.

His attention was caught by Gloria's door, and cutting short the conversation, he nodded in agreement. "Well, thanks. I guess we will have to wait and read it in the newspapers tomorrow."

That said, he walked toward her apartment and rang her bell, hoping she was awake and, most of all, alone.

He waited for a few seconds, and when he was ready to leave, the door opened ajar. She looked through it, wondering about her unexpected visitor.

When she saw Dave, she swung the door open and allowed him to come in without saying anything. She hurried to lock her door as if she feared something or someone.

"Are you okay?" he asked, observing the smooth curves of her body, hardly covered by the lace lingerie.

She took a deep breath, feeling glad to not be alone anymore. "Yes, I think I'm still shaken about last night's murder," she admitted, putting on her pink satin dressing gown.

Admiring her graceful figure slipping on the robe, he couldn't deny his growing attraction.

He shook his head, averting his gaze from her to focus on the reason for his visit. "What for? That was in the building in front of ours, and you weren't so scared last time when it happened here, and Johnny held you hostage," Dave wondered.

Gloria rolled her eyes. "Yeah, right, the boy was more frightened than me, and I know him. He's a good kid. When Spike got killed, it was only when Johnny reached his apartment and found him dead, when all hell broke loose. This time I was with a customer, and we both got startled by those repeated gunshots and the yelling of people. Haven't you heard anything?"

"No, I haven't. I'm a heavy sleeper; nothing wakes me up, besides the alarm clock."

"Good for you, but I'll never get used to it. I looked out the window, and there was quite a lot of people outside. Some residents of the building ran out onto the streets, fearing for their lives. Some mentioned a strange figure walking away from the crime scene," Gloria recalled, taking a seat on the couch.

"I've heard that too, but nobody could give me any specific information about it." Dave hoped she had more details to share with him.

"I haven't seen it," she brought a hand to her mouth, "but a friend of mine told me there was someone who didn't belong to any of the gangs ruling around here. You know, generally, their members are dressed wearing the colors of the gang, at least from what I understand. This one appeared to be a sort of lone wolf, according to her. He wore a dark coat."

Dave continued to think about it, almost concerned. His mind returned to that night, where he stumbled into the stranger, the man who went to visit Gloria.

"Do you have any idea who this person might be? Have you seen him before?" Gloria wondered as she acknowledged the change in his expression.

Dave shook his head, keeping his glance into the nothingness, trying to recall all the times he'd seen him. "I'm not sure about it, but I considered how bizarre it was. It came back to my mind that once I'd seen a guy coming here. He reminded me of Humphrey Bogart, and he came to your apartment. Could it be the same person?"

"Humphrey Bogart?" Gloria wondered, struggling to understand what he meant by that.

"Well, I don't know his identity, but he wore a coat with a fedora hat. I met him a few times as he came in or left from here," he explained. "However, it's been quite some time since the last time I've seen him."

"No, it's impossible." Gloria waved a hand, dismissing that comparison. "According to him, he left the country."

"Maybe he's his evil twin brother." His right brow arched in a semi-joking expression.

"You might have watched too many crime movies!" She stood from the couch. "Would you like something to drink? A coffee, perhaps?"

Not confident how he should answer, her tone reminded him of a person who was aware of more than she wanted to admit and tried to divert the discussion to another topic.

With an almost imperceptible grin, he decided not to get too deep into it, and keep his conclusions for himself. "It could be. You're probably right. Sometimes I get carried away by my imagination. That's something that often happens when you're used to being your best friend, and nobody can see you."

Gloria turned serious, slightly concerned for his introverted character, which gave him seemingly many problems in the social sphere. "How do you spend your free time?"

At her question, Dave tilted his head as if he didn't understand what she meant. "I-I like going jogging, and most of the time I don't have much free time, but I like drawing. My biggest dream was that of becoming a cartoonist for the newspaper. However, when I applied for the position, they needed an editor, and since I was qualified for the position, they hired me."

A bitter smile appeared on his face, as he also stood from the couch, walking to the window. "With time, I hoped this could be a way to get my foot in the door, but once a cartoonist job became vacant again, I applied for it. I wasn't lucky, or perhaps not skilled enough for it. So, I returned to my office, editing texts. I draw only on my free time, just for fun."

"Really?" Gloria smiled. "I want to have a look at some of your drawings, may I?"

Dave blushed. The only people he'd shown his work to were the recruiters at the newspaper, those who rejected him.

He'd been too shy to show his sketches to anyone else and didn't know how to react to her request. "My drawings are nothing worth mentioning. I have been turned down twice, so I'm afraid my value as a cartoonist is quite low if not zero." He lowered his gaze.

She came closer to him and raised his face to look into his eyes. "Why do you always have to be so negative? You should be the one who believes in yourself the most."

"That's true, but whether I do or not, there will never be anyone disposed to believe in me; I'm hopeless," Dave admitted.

"I do," Gloria kept her eyes steady on his, getting so close that he could smell the deodorant she'd been using that morning.

The faint essence curled up his lips in a smile. "Now, I'm curious, and I demand you to show me your sketches. Let me judge whether they are something I would like to see in a magazine, newspaper, or wherever else," she expressed, pushing him out of her apartment, walking toward Dave's.

"You will never accept 'no' for an answer, will you?" Dave wondered, amused.

"No, I never give up until I get what I want. Come on, let's go." She pushed him toward the door, impatiently waiting to see his art.

Dave hesitated in front of his door, trying to recall whether he might safely allow her to come inside his apartment without being embarrassed because of the disorder.

He mentally reviewed the whole place.

"What's going on?" Gloria wondered, puzzled by the way he literally froze.

He turned his gaze to her. "I'm trying to remember whether my place is presentable. I try to keep it tidied up, but sometimes I'm too lazy to put things in order."

"Don't you worry, my house isn't a temple of tidiness either. I'm not going to judge your housekeeping skills," she giggled, as she entered the apartment. Dave made a quick visual tour to ensure things were not as bad as he thought, and once again, he was surprised at his ability to keep the place ordered.

"What are you worrying about?" Gloria exclaimed open-mouthed, looking around herself. "This place is so cozy I would doubt it's the place of a bachelor. Last time I came here, it was a bit messy, to be honest, but now it's spotless."

"It happens that I do surprise myself too. I used to be more chaotic. Then one night, when I couldn't fall asleep, I started to clean up the place in a way I can't recall I've ever done before. Keeping it tidy is easier than I thought, and at times I feel like I still live in the old chaos." Dave shook his head.

"So, where are your drawings? I'm dying with curiosity," Gloria yelped excitedly.

His heart started to race in his chest as he walked to fetch his sketchbook, but before he opened it, he locked his eyes on hers. "Remember, I'm not a professional cartoonist, and for me, this is a hobby, so don't judge me too harshly."

Gently grabbing the book, she flashed a cunning smile. "Don't you worry, you will definitely be better than me, so I won't ever be in the position of judging anyone on their drawings." She started to flip through the pages, viewing the characters he'd been drawing, enchanted by the details and the perfection of those images.

Raising her eyes to look at him, she said, "My goodness, you got talent. They all seem so real."

"So, do you like them?" His face flushed at the compliment as he plunged his hands in his pockets. "Like them? I love them!" she exclaimed. "I cannot understand why they never accepted you."

"Perhaps this is a kind of style that wouldn't fit in a newspaper. Maybe it might be better in a comic book. My biggest problem is that I find it easy to draw different characters. Still, I can't write any storyline," Dave explained as she continued to observe his drawings.

"This is irrelevant. Generally, a writer takes charge of creating the story, and the artist is drawing. I read a lot of comics. I always see the name of the writer and the artist who drew it. You don't necessarily need to be able to do both," Gloria assured him, continuing browsing the pages.

"Thank you, I hope you think they're good."

"No-no-no, I've never said they're good – I said they're amazing, and you should think about getting your sketches to a publisher. I can understand why the newspaper refused you, and it's not an issue with your talent. This is the kind of material which fits better in a comic book," she smiled. "Have you ever tried sending your drawings to some publishing house where you can be appreciated?"

"You might be right, but I never showed them to anyone else. After I got rejected twice from my newspaper, I decided to be happy to have a decent job, rather than going through other rejections. However, as you say, I must admit this style wouldn't suit the comic strips in a newspaper. Perhaps, had I sent those to a comic book's publisher, they would have accepted it, and probably my life would have been different."

"Your work has nothing to do with your social life," warned Gloria, "it's all inside you, and not on what you do for a living. You could be the most famous TV character and be the loneliest person in the Universe."

Dave remained silent, thinking about it, and he thought she might have been right, but this brought him to the final conclusion that his life was doomed from the start.

There wasn't any easy solution to his problems. After all, he'd accepted his invisibility a long time ago.

To be honest, he felt almost comforted by that sort of foggy shield protecting him from the judgment of the rest of the world. He had to admit living in a world made of superheroes and fantasy wasn't bad. His characters never judged or bullied him.

They were his friends, and he gained something that, for many people, might seem a mirage: the full knowledge of the innermost part of his soul.

He wasn't a stranger to himself and didn't fear to go deep into his thoughts, exploring what was hidden in the deepest part of his heart.

Dave was at peace with himself; he still had Gloria's friendship to give him the feeling of being the luckiest man in the Universe.

He knew she would never be his girlfriend, but despite the soft spot he had for her since the beginning, he understood how lucky he was not to be completely alone.

Gloria made his life complete, and he didn't need to be in a relationship with her when he could count on her genuine friendship.

Perhaps having one good friend is far better than having a thousand fake friends, he thought as he watched her flipping the pages of his sketchbook.

"I'm not sure I need a social life. Most of the time, this means being surrounded by people who want to gain something from you. Even though I have only myself to offer, which isn't valued anymore as it was back in the old days, I'm blessed, for I have met a person like you," Dave admitted.

"I think I understand what you mean. Although you know I'm a prostitute, you never judged me and kept being my friend," Gloria glanced gratefully at him.

"I'll never forget your kindness..."

"You're talking like you're going somewhere," Dave observed.

"I'm not, but life is unpredictable, and we can't predict what tomorrow might bring."

Dave nodded. In his life, he'd never known unpredictability. He could count the sudden events in his life on the fingers of one hand.

There had been only a few unanticipated occurrences shaking his life.

First, was his father's death in a car accident, which shook the childhood away from his life, forcing him to see his existence under a new perspective.

The passing away of his mother by a long sickness afflicting her from a young age was something he had time to be prepared for.

Yet, having to say goodbye to the last living fragment of the family he was connected to, felt like becoming disconnected from the rest of the world.

His parents were perhaps the only ones who could see him. He was not invisible to them. Nevertheless, the most unforeseeable and incredible event in his life was meeting Gloria.

She shook his life and his whole world. He didn't care about how she earned her living; that wasn't anyone's business.

What really mattered was that since she entered his life, he found a new dimension, and his gray existence gained a few more colors.

"If you want, you can choose any of those drawings and keep it for yourself. You can take as many as you want. I draw almost every day," Dave proposed.

"Can I take what I want?" Gloria wondered, excited; she loved the way he drew.

"Sure, I'm not selling any of these, and if you like them, then there is no better place for them than in your closet or wherever you wish to keep them. Then, if one day we ever part, they will help you to remember me and our friendship," Dave ensured.

"I'm grateful for having met you. You're precious." Gloria smiled.

She took a quick look at them and chose three of them to keep for herself. "I think I'm in love with those three if you don't mind."

"You can take what you please; there is no restriction."

As she left the apartment, Dave thought about what he would do with the rest of his day.

The weather was quite gray, and he questioned whether he wanted to go to the park, but on the other hand, that would be the best way to clear his mind from all the recent happenings.

He glanced at the clock and considered having lunch right away and postpone the jog until the afternoon. "This would at least give me the chance to spend more time in the park, and perhaps the weather might even improve. Meanwhile, I'll cook and eat my meal," he declared.

He glanced at the sketchbook Gloria left on the table and flipped the pages of the drawings. He went through all the characters he'd been sketching there.

There were all his desires, fears, aspirations, and hopes; his whole soul was expressed within the lines impressed in the paper.

They were superheroes, villains, ordinary people, more or less successful, tragedies, and joys. He smiled and shook his head, placing the book on the table, then heading to the kitchen, trying to focus on what to eat.

In the afternoon, as he was jogging in the park, he thought about the last few months' events. The murders, particularly the strange figure spotted walking away from the crime scene, attracted his thoughts the most.

He wondered whether the man could have been connected to the homicide and if his identity would ever be revealed.

I would love to know if the police already know about this individual, or if they're on his tracks, trying to figure out his involvement with the murder.

What makes me curious is whether they will be able to connect the same person to Spike's death and the previous night's shooting. It seems like there's a lone avenger on the loose, and I'm wondering... He continued to jog until he was breathless and went to sit on a bench.

Regaining his breath, he looked around. There weren't many people walking in the park, like there generally were on Saturdays.

Dave pondered whether this was connected with the recent happenings. "Why have they started to fear for their safety only now?" he considered, talking to himself. "This neighborhood has been violent since forever. Why would these two new murders make any difference in people's perception of security? Besides, it seems like this mysterious guy is after those who jeopardize their safety; personally, I don't feel more threatened than before."

Not a single answer came to satisfy his questions. He wondered whether it was because of a presence they couldn't recognize or because of how it happened.

Grunting, he resumed his jogging, hoping to be able to start thinking about something else. The weather started to become even chillier as the winter advanced.

Knowing his body would have felt the cold amplified, he continued to run until he reached his apartment, to keep his body warm.

As soon as he closed the door behind him, he had one only desire – to get into a hot shower and relax.

The mysterious avenger inspired his creativity, and he decided to draw something about him. He spent the rest of the day drawing and figuring out the life a man like him would have.

Drawing that character made him wonder whether a person like that could ever be suspected of being the one behind those murders.

With a slight shake of his head, he released an amused chuckle. "People would never suspect an invisible gray man like me, and perhaps they would be right. Those things happen only in the movies and have nothing in common with real life."

Life in the neighborhood continued to flow with the same turbulence as usual. However, since the mysterious man didn't show up anymore, people seemed to believe he'd disappeared.

Other crimes grabbed the attention of the inhabitants away from the appearance of the lone avenger.

Drug dealers started to be warier of the people who approached them, but this was the only effect it had on the running of their business.

They felt safe enough of their power and security network to be convinced that they were still the owners of the area. Not only for what concerned their drug dealing but also as a free ground to unleash their terrorizing, violent behavior.

After dark, it was better for the honest and vulnerable ones not to be seen outside, as the gangs started to come out from their hiding places to return to their business.

The situation began to escalate when those night demons began to act during the day as well.

Everybody knew the police would take its time to reach any crime scene. That was particularly true when it was a question of the neighborhood where Dave lived.

He often thought about moving away to live somewhere else. Unfortunately, with his salary, he couldn't aim for much better areas, and making the effort of relocating to end up in a similar place was not something in his plans.

Moreover, now he had another reason to stay – Gloria. Even though she was a person who didn't need to be protected, he wasn't ready to abandon her.

In all likelihood, she could deal with her safety better than Dave himself, but he didn't want to be far from her either.

He didn't care when those people were killed during a clash between rival gangs; in his opinion, they got what they were looking for.

What he couldn't forgive was when they hurt innocent people. The only hope for him was to see the day when girls were able to go out without the fear of who was behind them.

He wasn't willing to accept having a young boy like Johnny killed or messed up by their game of power.

Nothing was excusable, but there wasn't anyone ready to risk their lives more than it was already to stand up and oppose the violence spreading.

That was the moment when people started to remember about the mysterious avenger, and perhaps they hoped he would be back to do the job the police were failing to do.

Nobody ever spoke aloud about this wish, but like whispers, it was passed from ear to ear, not wishing to be heard by anyone else, but hoping their pleas reached the avenger's ears.

Eventually, he decided to act one more time. In the end, this seemed to be something not destined to happen, but the voice continued to spread, like a buzz.

CHAPTER 4

It was on a mid-December morning, the swift approaching of Christmas holidays brought people in a jolly mood for the coming of one of the most awaited periods of the year.

To a certain extent, even criminals decided to take a break from their jobs and resume their activities after the holiday season.

However, as Dave returned from work, he realized immediately something wasn't right.

Opening the front door of his apartment building, he bumped against someone who was seemingly in a big hurry to move away.

The scent of his cologne filled his nostrils, and without apologizing, the man continued on his way.

Turning himself to see who the man was, he recognized the silhouette of the mysterious

Humphrey Bogart. "Wasn't he supposed to leave the country? What is he doing here, then?" His voice flickered.

Thousands of questions formulated in his mind as he watched him turning the corner connecting to the main road.

An uncomfortable sensation started to rise from his gut, like a premonition to a tragedy. "He never came to visit Gloria before sunset," he gasped, failing to notice the shortness of breath his racing heart caused.

Although Gloria didn't have a specific working schedule, five o'clock in the afternoon was a pretty unusual time for her to receive customers.

Clenching his fists, Dave hurried to climb the stairs, and as he reached the door of Gloria's apartment, he rang the bell without any hesitation.

When he got no answer, his knees seemed to fail him, and he leaned against the wall.

The visit of the mysterious man wasn't casual. He didn't drop by to say hello; that wasn't the way Gloria handled her customers.

Closing his eyes, he listened to his racing heart, trying to rationalize. "She might be out for some shopping, or wherever else. Perhaps he came to inform her he's back... As far as I know, he might have become a friend to her as I did."

Those explanations didn't reassure his soul and gathering his strength together he tried knocking at her door.

Surprise left him open-mouthed when it opened under the push of his knuckles. *What if he came to kill her?* Frozen and unable to move a step inside the now ajar door, fearing to enter and discover the lifeless body of the only real friend he ever had, he hesitated. *What if she's not dead yet? I might be in time to save her.*

With a sudden move, he slammed the door open and entered the apartment. He rubbed his eyes to make sure it wasn't a dream, nor was he hallucinating.

Like in a crazy nightmare where nothing follows any rational rule, the place was empty. Gloria had disappeared from the face of the Earth, bringing with her all her furniture, clothes, and personal effects.

Whatever was in her apartment the day before, had now literally vaporized. Feeling the room spinning, and being close to losing his consciousness, Dave staggered uncertainly, placing a hand against the wall to support his body.

His eyes toured the whole room in the hope of finding at least a clue. "I can't have been dreaming about her; I'm not hallucinating," he muttered the last word, rejecting the hypothesis of going crazy.

"No." He shook his head, covering his mouth with a hand. "That can't be a hallucination. She was real and lived right here. She also chose three of my drawings. I haven't imagined her, nor the guy who ran out from the door."

Those sketches were the only proof of her existence. Without a second thought, as if his life depended on it, he rushed like a maniac to his apartment, slammed the door open without caring about closing it behind him, and hurried to grab his sketchbook, flipping the pages to find the drawings he'd given away to Gloria.

As he remembered, they were missing, meaning they should be in Gloria's possession. Confident of not having imagined her, he returned to her apartment, searching more thoroughly for any sort of trace she might have left.

Starting from the living room, he went on systematically searching the whole house, without knowing what he was looking for.

A pin, a tissue, any evidence of her existence would have been enough; even one of her red hairs. He needed more proof of her being real.

A couple of hours were spent scanning every room, without any conclusive result. Hopeless, he sat on the floor and grabbed his head between his hands.

Not even the scent of the perfume she used remained. Nothing. She'd simply disappeared. His hands began to dampen with his tears filtering through his fingers, dripping to his jeans.

He wiped his eyes with the sleeve of his sweater, trying to get a hold of his emotions. "Now, I need to stay rational. If she's real, then someone must have seen her," he considered, focusing on who to ask.

The first person he thought about was the superintendent of the building. "He's the one who is aware of everything that's going on here, and he has the names of those people who move in or out," Dave spoke aloud to himself as he ran frantically to reach his office.

In front of the door of the superintendent's office, he hesitated, closing his eyes and listening to his heartbeat.

He waited for the right time to calm down and try to regain composure, and when he was confident of being in control of his emotions, he knocked on the door.

"Yes, come in," the thin voice of the superintendent, Mr. Jones, answered from his small office in the basement.

Dave went in, gingerly peeking from the fissure he'd opened. "Good afternoon, Mr. Jones, I'm sorry to disturb you, but I need some information about one of the residents of this building. At the number 35, at least until yesterday, lived a girl, but now the apartment is empty..."

The man glanced from his glasses placed at the tip of his nose, creasing his brow. "Number 35?"

"Y-Yes, her name is Gloria, but I can't recall her surname." Although, he'd known her a couple of months, he'd never asked her anything else but her first name.

He was also sure he never told her his own. Mr. Jones scratched his broad forehead and grabbed the register where all the documentation was stored.

He was an old man and opposed with all his strength to give in to the power of technology.

Proud of his resilience and having the chance to affirm that never in his life would a computer enter that room, he continued keeping the records of everything in large registers like they used to do ages ago.

With a smile, Dave wondered where he found those books for sale. "Well, let me take a look at it." He searched for the data of that apartment. "Oh, yes, she moved away," he chirped, after scrolling through all the names of the tenants.

A relieved exhale escaped Dave, as he acknowledged she wasn't a product of his overexcited fantasies, nor was he becoming crazy.

But then, why did she leave without a word? She hasn't even left a message in my mailbox, nothing at all, as if she wanted to disappear with the same speed, she arrived... I don't understand, there must be something more behind this move.

"Did she leave any address where she can be reached in case of need?"

"I mind my own business and didn't ask. She came here, gave me back the keys to be returned to the landlord, and left. I didn't ask, and she didn't say." He raised his hand as if to create a barrier to Dave's request.

"Can you at least tell me her surname?" Dave asked.

"This is a piece of information I can give; her name is Gloria Burroughs, but I cannot give you anything else, as those are classified details that pertain only to the police if they ask."

"I understand. I'm wondering why she had to leave without leaving a message or telling me her intentions," Dave muttered, talking to himself.

"This is none of my business, but perhaps she didn't want to tell anyone," Mr. Jones dared, narrowing his eyes.

"Hmm..." Dave grunted. "Well, maybe this is the reason why, but thanks for your information."

"You're welcome," Mr. Jones replied as he left the office.

Something still doesn't fit. Why, for example, was the door of the apartment open if she returned the key to the superintendent, and what did Humphrey Bogart come for? Was it a coincidence, or did he have something to do with her departure? His mind struggled to find an answer to all the questions swirling in his soul, biting his lower lip until it bled.

However, no matter how hard he tried, his mind switched to a blank screen. He glanced once again at the door of the apartment where Gloria lived for the past two months.

I don't believe she was forced to leave because of her job, nor that the police arrested her. Why would they? He opened the door and entered the apartment. *She must have left something behind, something that can give me any clue about the place where she has moved to.*

Without knowing what to look for, he kept looking around every corner of the empty place.

In his mind, he was sure that once he found it, it would clear up everything in that mystery.

Just like the last piece in a puzzle, it could give him a fundamental clue about where Gloria was. "What if I ask the police? Although she's not missing, something doesn't fit in this story. Perhaps an invisible man can find a way to become visible, for once, and obtain help from the police," he pondered, as he was sure of having searched the whole place without leaving any corner unsearched.

He returned to his apartment, thinking about a way to ask for assistance. "I don't want to appear like a stalker who has lost track of his target. They would, for sure, ask Mr. Jones and the other residents. According to Mr. Jones, she moved away, although he admitted it was an unexpected move. Eventually, she left an address, but I'm the one who appeared in his office asking for her name and surname, and where to find her. A woman that runs away from the place where she lives might be forced by a stalker or a violent relationship," he said aloud. "For sure, they will open an investigation on my friendship with Gloria, and perhaps they will decide I'm her stalker."

He collapsed on his couch, trying to find a solution to his problems.

Indeed, he acknowledged the absence of any proof, which indicated he harassed her; actually, there hasn't been a case on him, yet he felt like they were judging him.

A low-pitched noise caught his attention, a sound like someone tried to ask for help. It was a soft, muffled cry.

Jumping to his feet like a spring, he rushed to open the window from his bedroom, which faced the road. He turned his head in both directions.

Not being able to have a complete vision of the street, he didn't wait any longer and ran outside, trying to find out whether he could find the place where it came from, but everything returned to silence as soon as he got out.

He was almost home, the same muffled cry he heard before, apparently coming from one of the sides of the building where secondary roads led to the backside where the parking area was located, caught his attention.

Dave ran toward the noises and as he arrived at the parking lot, he saw Shauna, the daughter of one of the families living on the second floor.

Together with her were a couple of guys, those who believed the whole place belongs to them.

Obviously, they were the only ones who were enjoying the meeting.

"Let her go!" Dave yelled at the top of his lungs, not understanding what to do to help her, if not offering his life in exchange for her safety.

The two guys looked at him, surprised, but as he came into the light, they froze, like they'd seen the devil itself, a ghost, or everything together.

They didn't say anything; they ran away, leaving Shauna sobbing on the ground.

Dave remained for a moment, dumbfounded at their reaction and wondered what scared them so much to put them on the run that way.

He walked to the girl and hugged her. "Shauna, are you hurt?"

She went on crying and held herself to him, unwilling to let him go. "That's okay, sweetie," he added in a lower tone of voice.

"Now, let's go back to your family where you'll be safe." Without saying another word, he lifted her in his arms and started walking back to her apartment.

This isn't a place to raise children, but on the other hand, if you don't have another place to go, what are you supposed to do? He thought as he climbed the stairs to the second floor.

Dave lowered her to stand on her feet and glanced at her. "You should tell your parents about what happened today. They must call the police."

"Why call them when you're around?" She wiped her tears, glancing at him in awe like she was talking to some sort of Superman.

"Because I might not be there next time. It was by chance that I heard your voice. Had I been out or sleeping or whatever else, your cry would have gone unnoticed. Also, those people need to be brought to jail," Dave tried to explain.

"If it weren't you, perhaps it would have been the mysterious avenger." Her voice lowered as if she was talking about a supernatural being. "Everybody is gossiping about him; besides, the police come here only when someone is dead. I prefer being saved than having my corpse collected somewhere."

Shauna smiled weakly, still shaken by what happened.

"Let me ask you one thing," Dave touched the base of his neck. "I don't think I look so threatening, so why did those two thugs look at me like they saw a ghost?"

Biting her lower lip, she looked at him through a lowered glance. "There's a rumor about you. They say you're the mysterious avenger; they also say so..." Shauna revealed.

"What?!" Dave exclaimed, interrupting him. "What avenger? I haven't killed anyone, nor have I any intention of doing that. Who is spreading this kind of rumor about me?"

He paced nervously along the corridor, wiping his hair back. His heart started to race as panic took over his self-control.

He'd never asked for a place in the spotlight, and most certainly not under the name of a killer.

Shauna looked at him and wondered why he was so scared about it. *Maybe it's because he wants to keep the anonymity. Yet, I don't understand; he should be glad to be considered a hero,* she thought.

"Listen..." she continued, trying to calm him down, but then she realized she didn't know his name.

"Yes, exactly, nobody knows my name, even though I've been living in this building for at least ten years. My life has been a constant gray existence where I was almost sure to be invisible to the rest of the world. Now, suddenly, because someone decided to do justice on his own, I've become the one who is going to solve the problems of the whole world. Then Gloria..." Words failed him.

The only certain thing was that he found himself in the middle of a mess from which he had no idea how to get out.

"I'm sorry, nevertheless, whatever your name is, people believe in you. You don't need to be the avenger. You represent the hope they cannot find in the police, and the fact that those guys ran away scared means a lot to everyone. Can't you pretend to be the mysterious avenger?" Her forehead creased and she grinned.

Dave looked in her eyes and understood what she meant.

However, regardless of the need for people to have something to believe in, he didn't want to be associated with any criminal activity, which might have landed him in prison for multiple murders. "Shauna, you're too young to understand, but if this story reaches the ears of the police, I'll be in trouble," he explained. "By the way, my name is Dave."

Shauna pouted. "I get it. Let's make it this way: I will always be ready to testify in your favor, and together with me, all the other people who need to have a hero."

"What if instead those thugs come and kill me? Who is going to save me?" Dave spread his arms, hoping to make her realize the dangers behind that plan. Shauna remained silent for a moment, trying to find a solution.

"You're right and I'm sorry. However, I'm not the person who gossips about you being the avenger. Some people swear having seen you at every crime scene since Spike got killed. I have no idea how this rumor came out, and I can't stop it, because I'm only a teenage girl, and they barely listen to me when I say something."

"Well, then don't mention me at all in regard to what happened today, but you need to tell your parents about those guys," Dave insisted, trying to figure out a way to make those rumors stop.

"What am I supposed to say, then?"

"Tell them a car came, surprising them, and you were able to run away. You don't need any reason to find a hero in every situation, and I'm the least suitable person to be one." His voice sounded with an echo through the walls of the empty corridor.

For a moment, he listened to his voice, returning to his ears and couldn't believe he was in the position to defend himself from the suspicion of being a superhero.

"In case I haven't made it clear, you ARE a hero; you didn't think for a second whether they would have killed you or not. You came to save me when I needed the intervention of someone. But don't you worry, I'll keep your secret." She winked, amused, and ran toward her apartment. "By the way," she turned her gaze at him, "thank you for saving my life by risking yours."

With those words, she opened the door and disappeared inside without waiting for an answer from Dave.

For a moment, Dave remained frozen with his mind completely blank. Everything seemed to conspire against his invisibility, and even though it had never been his choice, now he was missing it.

His life became more and more complicated with the passing of the days. *A hero,* he pondered as he started to walk toward the stairs to reach his apartment. *I did what anyone in my place would have done. I never could have allowed Shauna to be raped or killed, she's only a little girl! What kind of monster wouldn't go to help her?*

He shook his head, but then he recalled that he was the only one who ran out of his apartment, trying to locate her and wondered about those who preferred to remain safely inside their houses.

A tear fell from his eye as he went inside. "Most likely, they thought about their safety more than Shauna's. People are terrified, and I was reckless when I ran out without thinking about my own security."

He tried not to think about what happened anymore and hoped Shauna didn't mention him to her parents.

He still needed his invisibility to find out Gloria's location and whether she was in trouble. "Perhaps we really need a hero, but I'm not one. I want to do the right thing, and now I need to make sure Gloria is safe and sound, wherever she might be," he whispered. "The presence of that man in a coat and fedora makes me think something has happened to her; she didn't leave..."

Meanwhile, in the building and the whole neighborhood, the word started to spread of what happened to Shauna.

She tried to keep the secret and indeed she didn't confirm the fact that Dave was the avenger, but it was enough for everybody to know that he ran without hesitation to save her to make him a hero in the eyes of the residents.

Unfortunately, these rumors also spread to those who lived their lives on the illegal side of the law, and they were not happy about what happened in the parking lot.

It was not that someone saved the girl from rape, but the suspicion that he might be related to the murder of a few of them.

The fact that they were not sure about his identity played in Dave's favor, as none of them thought of getting rid of him.

Nevertheless, they were determined to keep an eye on him, to make sure nobody would intrude in their business.

It was dinner time when someone knocked at Dave's door. Until that moment the only visits he'd received were that of the postman and Mr. Jones.

He never had any friends coming by and his neighbors didn't even know his name, at least those who acknowledged his presence. He thought about it for a moment, but when they knocked a second time, he walked to the door hesitatingly. "Who's there?"

"I'm Shauna's mother. Please, open the door?" a female voice pleaded from the other side of the door.

Dave rolled his eyes, knowing Shauna couldn't keep her mouth shut. *What can I expect from a teenager?* He opened the door and tried to smile, as he felt his hands damp with sweat. "Ehm... good evening."

"Hi," the woman averted her gaze from him, trying to find a place to focus her attention. "Shauna told me what happened. I wanted to tell you how thankful I am for your bravery. Many people would have pretended not to hear her because those guys do not have any respect for life. You might think you haven't done anything special, but..."

Her tears suffocated her breath, and she started to sob hopelessly. Mrs. Dora Parker was Shauna's mother.

Everybody knew her husband died a few years ago, but luckily, the job at the grocery store provided enough money for them.

Dora looked like she'd stepped out of an old picture. Determined to the bone to reach whatever goals she had in mind, and since the birth of Shauna, that meant giving her all the tools to be able to get a good job and leave that neighborhood.

Her only hope was to have her daughter safe and sound. Concerning herself, she was happy with her job and didn't need anything fancy in her life.

Her family had never been wealthy, but the way they stick together, taking care of each other, was the most valuable treasure.

Remarrying or even dating another man wasn't included in her plans. "I had one husband who I deeply loved and respected. God took him away from me to have him in his glory, and there is no other I'll ever think about for the rest of my life until we will be reunited," she used to say.

Her sister came from time-to-time to visit her for a few weeks. She lived far away, and she didn't have the possibility to entertain herself more than those holidays every year.

Despite that, they kept in touch by phone and if possible, their relationship got stronger even with those endless miles dividing them.

Mrs. Parker had always had the desire to travel to her sister, but her salary didn't allow her. Moreover, all her savings were meant to serve as her retirement money and for Shauna's college.

Being an invisible presence gave Dave the opportunity to get in touch with the life and times of most of the people living in his apartment building.

Besides being a curse, it also represented an advantage, which the latest events brought into jeopardy.

Not knowing what he was supposed to do or how to behave in this particular case, he invited her inside.

He thought that perhaps she would feel more comfortable being in a private place rather than crying in the corridor. "Please, Mrs. Parker, I did what I had to, and to be honest I acted by instinct without thinking. Had I thought a bit more, maybe I would have done like many others. Although I'm glad that I acted the way I did," Dave tried to calm her.

"Don't you realize it? You know the names of everybody here, and we don't even acknowledge your existence. I feel ashamed about this." She struggled to regain control over her emotions.

Dave invited her to sit down on the couch and offered her a glass of water.

"Thanks," she breathed, adjusting her skirt as she sat on the couch. "Rape is an experience that destroys lives. I can't think about the consequences that could have had on my Shauna."

She took a deep breath as she tried to swallow the tears that twinkled in her eyes. "If there is something I hope for her, it's to complete her studies and leave this place as soon as possible. I wish only the best for her and you gave her another chance. Without you, her life would not have been the same anymore. I owe the fact that she can smile with the same brightness as usual to your bravery, and whenever you need anything you don't have to do anything else but ask," she concluded, locking her eyes on him.

"Mrs. Parker, I'm glad I helped Shauna, and I hope from now on she will be more careful when she's coming back home. However, I might have a question for you, but I don't know whether you have an answer," Dave tried to explain.

"If there is anything I can do to help you, I'll do it gladly." She beamed at him.

"Do you remember the girl who lived in the apartment at the end of this corridor? She was a beautiful young girl with red hair..."

"Oh... you mean the prostitute." Her expression toughened.

"Her name is Gloria," Dave corrected. "However, from one second to another she disappeared, vaporized like thin air, and I'm wondering whether she has been threatened by someone, and she was forced to move away. I'm worried, and I hope nothing bad has happened to her."

Mrs. Parker inhaled deeply, relaxing a bit. "I have seen her perhaps a couple of times, and we never talked to each other. I thought she decided to leave because of the complaints she received from the other tenants. It wasn't nice to have that traffic of her customers around here..."

"I wasn't aware of those quibbles," he mumbled, leaning on the armchair, scratching his chin. "Honestly, I haven't heard anything coming from her apartment. We became friends, and we went out for a beer from time-to-time, but nothing else. She was the one who could see me and talked to me in the whole neighborhood, if we exclude Mr. Jones," Dave admitted.

Mrs. Parker lowered her gaze, understanding that perhaps a prostitute was more ready to see through the gray existence of Dave's and acknowledge his presence.

That was something all the other 'decent' people failed in. Dave didn't want to create any discomfort. "You don't have to feel ashamed for not being aware of me all these years. I have to admit this is a problem many others share, and perhaps Gloria was one in a million. Since I was born, it has been almost impossible for the rest of the world to acknowledge my presence. That happened at school and everywhere else; sometimes also at home, so don't feel bad about it. I'm used to being invisible." Dave knew his use of that word was perhaps a bit excessive, but the fact that people failed to notice him, whether it was his or their fault, gave him the conviction that he was invisible.

"Our world is going too fast, and in one way or another we're all undetectable to each other. My daughter was invisible to all those who preferred to keep themselves safe, rather than helping her.

Perhaps only an invisible hero like you could overcome the fear of being killed to save Shauna. I'll never forget what you have done for us, and if anything about Gloria comes to my mind, I'll let you know," she stood from the couch.

"I appreciate your effort. I'm also considering asking the police, but I'm afraid they might misinterpret my desire to find her." Dave hesitated.

"How could they misinterpret it?" Mrs. Parker wondered, stopping on her way to the door.

Dave felt almost ashamed to admit his thoughts and perhaps he was a bit paranoid, but a second opinion might help him find the right solution. "I'm afraid that, since I'm only a friend, they would think I've been stalking her and now that I've lost track of her, I'm asking the police to help me find my victim."

"Nonsense!" Mrs. Parker exclaimed with a giggle. "Why would they think you're a stalker? This description could fit one of her customers, not you. You're a decent person who cares about everybody."

Dave nodded. "Perhaps you're right, and I should think about asking for their help."

She smiled and strode toward the door. "I hope you will be able to find her and that she left because of the complaints she received rather than because of a threat. But if you care, I suggest you go and ask for the help of the police."

"Speaking of the police," Dave recalled, "you should inform them about what happened to Shauna. I understand you prefer to keep a low profile, but until we all do so, the children in this neighborhood will be in danger, not to mention all the other people. Also, Shauna got lucky this time, but next time, if I'm not there ready to intervene..."

Mrs. Parker cringed. "If I go to the police and give them the names of the guys who tried to rape my daughter, they will get revenge on me and particularly on Shauna. If I don't do anything, they will continue as they did so far... I have no idea what I'm supposed to do. It appears like whatever I do, we will all be in trouble."

Her voice flickered like the flame of a candle.

"You need to think about it, and I won't take any action until you ask me to do so. However, doing nothing will help no one. You can't live your life hoping Shauna will be safe until she goes to college or she has the chance to leave this place," Dave warned.

Mrs. Parker nodded thoughtfully, opening the door of the apartment. "I'll think about it. Thank you once again."

"You're welcome. Take care." Dave watched her walking away.

He closed the door and started to think about the chat he had with her. He thought about what she told about the other tenants complaining about Gloria's presence.

"How could they complain when she was as discreet as possible?" he considered. "I understand many people would consider her lifestyle morally unacceptable, but if we think only about her business, she had a carefully selected clientele, and there hadn't been noises or any other sort of trouble."

Despite being at home every evening, most of the time, he never noticed anything that could have been interpreted as a disturbance. "I wonder why she never talked to me about this problem," he said as he was preparing his dinner. "Unless Mr. Jones collected all the complaints and asked her to leave as soon as possible in the name of the other tenants."

He sighed and decided to focus his attention on his food and take care of going to the police as soon as he found the guts to do it, possibly the following day.

CHAPTER 5

Running down the stairs, as he reached the second floor of his apartment building on his way to go to work, his gaze was caught by the mailboxes lined at the entrance.

He couldn't recall having checked his own mailbox for at least a week. So many things had happened to make him almost forget about it.

Usually, he didn't receive anything important except the commercial fliers of the shops. Yet, he was surprised to see a folded letter, together with the usual ads.

His heart sank as he unfolded it, and he realized he was holding one of the sketches he gave to Gloria.

Under the drawing, a message was added: *'I'm sorry...'*

That piece of paper he held in his trembling hand wasn't just proof she was alive, it proved that something, or someone, forced her to leave in such a hurry not to allow her to tell him goodbye.

In his eyes, her apology sounded like a request for help; something she couldn't even fathom was after her and had terrified her.

If it were a pondered decision, she would have come to his apartment, explaining the reason why she intended to move away.

Leaving a message that way, using a sketch she chose to keep, meant she had no time to search for a piece of paper to write him a note.

He considered that if she'd had the time, she could have better explained her decision, but that *'I'm sorry'* gave him a different version about how the events unfolded.

Concern and confusion darkened his expression and, in a final attempt to reorganize his thoughts, he wondered whether he should call the newspaper and take the day off. "I need a better excuse to take a day off at the last moment. Besides, I need something else to focus on to clear my mind. The only reason not to show up was being brought to the hospital after an accident, but that wasn't the case."

He traced his steps back and forth a couple of times, before resuming his walk to his job.

Although he considered it an emergency, he could wait to get out of the office to go to the police to show them the message she left.

I wonder whether I can ask my supervisor to leave earlier so I can reach the Police Station and talk with someone about this, he pondered, keeping his eyes on the ground, focused only on his thoughts.

Considering the possibility reasonable enough, he rushed to the newspaper, determined to solve the situation first thing in the morning.

As soon as he reached his office, he took off his coat, and even before starting up his computer, he strode to the office of his supervisor.

After a moment of slight hesitation, furrowing his brows, he knocked at the door. "Yes," Mr. Johnson growled.

He gently pushed open the door and cautiously entered the room. "Good morning," he closed the door behind him.

"Oh, good morning, Dan." Mr. Johnson smiled amiably.

"Ehm... I'm Dave," he corrected, lowering his gaze.

"Oh well, whatever. Tell me, what can I do for you?"

Disheartened by his careless behavior, he grimaced. "I was wondering whether I can take a few hours off today. I need to go to a check-up and getting out earlier would help me to reach the doctor's office without being stuck in traffic." His heart started to race as he twisted his entwined fingers.

Mr. Johnson remained silent for a moment. "Well, I think this is something you can do if you manage to finish the most urgent tasks for today. Hopefully, everything will be fine. Take care of yourself."

"I hope so too, thanks." That was only half a lie, as he really needed to book a visit to a doctor as soon as possible.

His ability to fall asleep had deteriorated with the recent events. "Your job requires you to be as sharp as a pencil; we cannot afford to release a poorly edited piece."

A broad smile appeared on Mr. Johnson's face, something quite rare to see.

With the same euphoria as a man who won the lottery, Dave nodded frantically, "Indeed, thank you. I'll go back to my office and get everything done for this early afternoon."

"Perfect, have a nice day!" Mr. Johnson wished as Dave left the room.

After a double cup of coffee, he rushed to his office and started to immerse himself in his work.

An unusual amount of texts to be edited waited for him, but he was determined to complete it before three o'clock, even if this meant sacrificing his lunch break.

It was supposed to be a good day, as never in his life had he been more focused, and motivated in his tasks.

To his surprise, he realized at three in the afternoon, he'd also had the time to double check everything and, satisfied with the results, he could leave as agreed with his supervisor.

Walking the streets, reaching the underground station, he started to think about the way to approach the topic at the Police Department.

When someone disappears, a family member would usually report the missing person, but according to what she told him, her family turned their backs on her.

But is this the case? I know she left in a hurry, and perhaps she also gave her new address to Mr. Jones, who didn't share it with me to protect her privacy, he thought.

That didn't surprise him, considering the career she'd chosen for herself, but family should stick together no matter what.

Besides, she didn't harm anyone, and although prostitution is considered immoral, at least in her case it was a conscious choice. "I personally think she's a sweet person, and I don't care about the way she earns her living. The only thing I want is to make sure she's not in danger," his voice trembled as he reached the Police Station.

In the lobby, he hesitated one last time, wondering where he was supposed to go and what he was supposed to ask.

Nevertheless, he decided to start from the most obvious place, the information desk.

"Good afternoon, how can I help you?" the girl asked, smiling kindly at him.

"Good afternoon, I hope so. I need to find the right department," Dave commenced. "A few months ago, a girl moved to the apartment next door. However, a couple of days ago, she disappeared without leaving a trace. I also asked the superintendent, but he couldn't help me. Recently, a few murders have been committed, and during one of these she had been held hostage, but she didn't press charges against the offender. Nevertheless, I believe there is something bigger behind this sudden move..."

He'd been quite verbose in his explanation; that often happened when he was under stress or afraid of something.

There wasn't anything he could do to help it; once his mouth opened, those words would flow out of his soul like a river.

I hope she won't consider me a lunatic.

The girl looked at him, trying to make any sense out of his blurting, and thinking which department was better to send him. "I'm not sure but it might be a case of a missing person, but they can tell you with more accuracy."

Dave nodded, wondering whether he should also add the detail of the message he'd received in his mailbox. *Oh well, I think I can tell the officer later*, he pondered as he walked to the floor where such cases were handled.

As he arrived at the waiting room for his turn, he started to doubt this was anything that pertained to the police, and perhaps it was a job for a private investigator, but that kind of service required more money than he'd ever earned in his life.

He sighed, and when it was his turn to talk to the officer, his doubts became almost unbearable.

"Good afternoon, tell me what the problem is," the officer said.

Dave started to explain and showed him the message she left for him. He tried to put an emphasis on every detail of the story, but it seemed like he was not impressed.

"Admittedly, the situation is indeed suspicious, but this woman isn't definitely missing," he doubted, thinking about the right place to direct Dave.

"Well, I cannot find her, at least," Dave bit his lips as if to withdraw his words.

A chuckle escaped him. "The fact that you can't find her doesn't mean something has happened to her. However, it's strange to leave suddenly from one day to another without any trace. Where was she working?"

Dave wasn't sure he could tell him she was a prostitute. He didn't want to create more problems for her than she already had.

Nevertheless, this could have also opened the possibility of violence against her. He decided to keep this detail to himself, at least until they opened a case, and he could talk with the detective in charge of the investigation. "I think she was still looking for a job when she moved in the apartment," he tried to lie, hoping to be convincing enough.

"Okay," he handed him a questionnaire. "Please, fill out this form as carefully as possible. I'll hand it to the Detective Bureau and if they decide she's a missing person, rather than a woman who decided to leave the city for her own personal reasons, they will open a case, and if needed, they will ask you for more information."

Dave grabbed the form and filled it out with all the required information. He doubted they would contact him.

In his experience, the police never cared about people living in his neighborhood, because there were too many issues to solve, and they could not reserve all their manpower to handle places like that.

He was conscious of the problems with the crime rate in that part of the city. Yet, also for this reason he considered it highly unfeasible that he would be contacted by anyone who would care about what happened to Gloria.

He memorized the name and surname of the officer he'd been speaking with and if within a couple of days he hadn't heard from anybody, he'd call them one more time, pushing as much as he could to start the investigation.

"So, this is it?" he wondered as he handed back the filled questionnaire. With a quick glance at the completed form, the officer raised his gaze at him and smiled.

"Yes, that will be enough. Although I need to warn you; cases like this rarely require the intervention of the police. People move away from their homes quite often, and it doesn't warrant any reason for us to use manpower in an investigation. As I mentioned, nobody leaves in such a hurry without a good reason, but we need more evidence in order to judge it as a possible case of stalking, kidnapping, or anything else."

His expression toughened as he warned of an eventual negative outcome. "So, you need to see the girl killed, before you'll do anything to help her..." His voice was just a whisper, meant to be heard only by himself.

He thanked the officer and stood, lazily resuming his steps back to the exit, where he would take the first train back home.

"I hope I won't need to call them one more time to force them to do their job, but I need to know what happened to Gloria. I'm not going to accept the fact that she left, without a more plausible explanation than the strange message," he muttered on his way home.

He had just stepped inside his apartment when his telephone started to ring, displaying a number he didn't recognize.

"Dave Stanford," he answered absentmindedly, as he took off his coat and shoes, getting more comfortable.

"Good evening Mr. Stanford, this is Officer Kane Orwell of the Detective Bureau. Earlier this afternoon, you filed a case for a missing person, correct?"

Dave was dumbfounded at hearing the detective's voice. He was sure it would have taken much longer for the police to contact him regarding Gloria going missing.

"Yes," Dave mumbled, "I wasn't expecting your call so early. To be honest, I believed you would never call me."

"Why wouldn't I?" Dave's answer surprised him.

"Well, I live in an area where crime is like daily bread. Police don't intervene very often. This isn't meant to criticize your actions; I know you can't solve the crimes happening in every part of the city and municipality, but I feared this case was destined to be archived." Dave squeezed in his shoulders.

Officer Orwell was surprised by his frank answer, but Dave was right, and they didn't have the resources to take care of every crime perpetrated in their jurisdiction.

"I understand your feelings, but that's the chance you were waiting for, and I hope we will find Ms. Burroughs as soon as possible and alive," Officer Orwell's voice turned into a growl. "I would like to meet you to gather all the information. When do you think you could stop by the Detective Bureau?"

"Wouldn't it be better if you came here, so I can also show you the apartment where Gloria lived? In this case you can start to get an idea of the neighborhood," Dave proposed.

"Do you work in security?" Officer Orwell wondered.

"No, I'm an editor at the newspaper, and in my free time I draw, so nothing connected with security services of any kind." An amused chuckle escaped Dave.

"Well perhaps you might consider it," Officer Orwell chuckled, entertained by Dave's eagerness. "I'll be there within an hour, and we will talk about the case and you can show me around."

"I'll be waiting for you." Dave's face flushed at the fact of being not just seen but considered. "You know my address."

"Yes, I do; see you soon," Officer Orwell hanged up the conversation abruptly.

Dave frowned, glancing at the telephone. Shrugging his shoulders, he mumbled, "Sure, bye."

Looking around his apartment, he needed to get used to seeing the house in order yet. He decided to use the waiting time to take care of the smallest details in there, so as not to be ashamed of receiving guests in an improper mess. Just as soon as he was satisfied with the state of his apartment, someone rang at the door.

During the day, the front door of the building remained open to the public, mainly because the building hosted a few commercial activities for which it would be awkward having it locked to their customers.

Dave took a deep breath and opened the door. The man standing on the other side didn't resemble the idea Dave had depicted in his mind.

He wore the jacket of the police uniform and a pair of jeans.

Officer Orwell was a man in his forties, perhaps slightly overweight, with a charming way of glancing at people.

Although he was shorter than Dave, a fire burned in his dark eyes that could strike fear. A self-confidence transpired from his general being, which Dave could only dream of.

For a second, he didn't move, scrutinizing Officer Orwell from head to toe, as if in his mind, he'd already decided he was the Humphrey Bogart man.

That is the damage made by the Hollywood movies; they give you a false image of reality, Dave thought.

The officer had a way of looking at others like he was going to penetrate their minds, trying to discover all their darkest secrets.

He could force them to confess, and before they even knew it, Officer Orwell had brought them to jail.

"Good evening," Officer Orwell noticed Dave's reticence. "Do you think it would be safe for me to come in, or do you think I should stay out?"

Dave smiled, relaxing a bit. "Of course, Officer. I still find it strange that you reached out for me to start the investigation. I'm sorry, please come in. May I offer you anything? A coffee?"

"No, thank you, perhaps one day when I'm not on duty. Now, I want only to get a clearer picture of the situation," he took out an agenda book from his pocket.

Without waiting for the invitation to do so, Officer Orwell took a seat on the couch. "I need everything you got about this girl, Gloria Burroughs. Was she your girlfriend, or did you have any sort of relationship besides the normal friendship?"

"No, we were only friends." Dave hesitated.

"Did she have any boyfriend or any other relationship? Family?"

"As far as I know her family turned their backs on her. I believe it was because of her choices in life that put them apart."

Officer Orwell glanced Dave with a suspicious look. "I'm not here to investigate based on guesses.

I'm here only to find this girl. My impression is that you're trying to hide something from me, and I need to warn you, whatever you're hiding won't help me in any way. You need to be totally honest."

Dave backed up and felt like a child who has been caught red-handed by his mother. "I... well, she's a prostitute, and she used to select her customers online and receive them here in her apartment."

He hoped he was not going to give Gloria more trouble than she already had, he only meant to help her and to understand what was going on.

"You see? It wasn't so difficult, and this information is going to be vital to choose the lead, and the direction where to search for her. Now, did you notice any particular person among her customers who could be connected with her disappearance? Any detail could be important."

"I'm not sure, but a few days after she moved in, I saw a man frequenting her apartment quite regularly before she disappeared. What grabbed my attention was the way he dressed. He had a light brown coat and a fedora hat, which made me think about Humphrey Bogart in the movie Casablanca," Dave recalled. "I've never seen his face, and when I asked her about him, she assured he moved away from the country. However, I recall the day when I discovered that Gloria left, I crossed him at the front door. I thought he returned and searched for her, but since he found the apartment empty, he decided to leave..."

"But you suspect he might have a role in Gloria's disappearance, don't you?" Officer Orwell asked as he continued to write notes in the agenda book without even raising his glance to Dave.

"Certainly, he was the only customer I saw coming to her place after she left. This made me think that she had the time to inform her customers, either by email or other means about her departure. However, I knew she worked only by appointment, so if this Humphrey Bogart guy was a regular customer, he should have called her, and would have been aware of her departure," Dave considered.

"Well, if she had been kidnapped or something happened to her, this might not be possible. Yet, his presence is suspicious. I'll need to search for him." Officer Orwell rubbed the stubble on his chin. "Can you give me any other details?"

"Probably this isn't connected in any way, but recently the cases of murder in this neighborhood increased.

But whereas before, the victims were people who resisted a robbery, victims of rape who went to the police, and so on, now it seemed like some sort of avenger appeared to kill the bad guys.

People around here talk about a man in a dark coat who has been spotted at the crime scenes, but I haven't seen him, so I can't say whether he's real or a tale. Gloria told me about him," Dave recalled.

"So, let me get this straight: Ms. Burroughs arrives here, and this strange guy starts to visit her with a certain regularity. At the same time, a mysterious avenger also appears to eliminate members of the local criminals," Officer Orwell muttered as he continued to scribble in his book. "So, it seems like this 'Humphrey Bogart' has a wicked twin brother, or they're the same person, or they're both evils." A grin appeared on his face.

"According to those who live here, the avenger is a sort of hero. He's taking care of the safety of the innocent more effectively than the police have done so far," Dave dared sarcastically.

"Hero or not, we need to know whether there is any connection between these three people. Can you show me the place where Ms. Burroughs lived?" he asked.

"Of course." Dave stood from the couch. "Follow me. It's right at the end of this corridor."

They both left Dave's home and reached the door of Gloria's former apartment. "Here is the place."

He tried to push the door and unexpectedly, it opened, like nobody ever cared to lock it. "Who is the owner of this apartment? Has he been informed about the vacancy?" Officer Orwell wondered, surprised to find the place open.

"For this, you should ask Mr. Jones. He's working here as a superintendent, and he knows everything about what's going on in this building; at least this is what he's supposed to do. I guess he had to contact the owner and return the keys to the apartment. Evidently, either he forgot, or the owner didn't show up to get the keys..." Dave presumed.

"Maybe the landlord has a role in the disappearance of Ms. Burroughs," Officer Orwell proposed, as he peeked inside the place. "It seems like, although she left in a hurry, she had time to remove everything and clean it as if there had never been anyone living here, which makes me think that someone wanted to delete every single trace of her presence," Officer Orwell mumbled as if he was talking to himself. "Did you come inside this apartment before?" Officer Orwell asked, turning to talk to Dave.

"Yes, I was curious about what had happened and whether I could find something to give me a sort of indication about her location, but I haven't touched anything. I walked around, so I guess there is only the print of my shoes," Dave hoped he didn't do anything stupid.

"Why didn't you call us immediately?"

"I was afraid to be suspected of her disappearance." His voice reached a lower tone, understanding how foolish that sounded.

Narrowing his eyes and locking his glance on Dave to understand what he was hiding and what his role in that story was, he asked, "Would we have any reason for it? Did you argue with her in a way to raise suspicion?"

"No, I panicked. I never found myself in this kind of situation, and I was confused about what I was supposed to do. I knew I should call you before..."

Perfect, if before I feared to be included in the list of the suspects, now he will be sure about my possible involvement. Why in the heck did I have to be so stupid? Dave wondered, wishing to be able to punch himself on the face.

"I'm not suspecting you of her missing, don't you worry, although you should have contacted us earlier. I don't think you're involved in this case, but from this moment on, I wish for your full cooperation, and I hope I'll gather enough information about her from the other tenants of this building," Officer Orwell smirked. "I wouldn't be that sure about them."

"Why?"

"Because they don't trust a policeman. They consider you too far from their problems, and perhaps they think you're also one of the causes of their problems," Dave admitted openly.

He didn't know from where he got the guts to speak aloud that way to an officer. "We're not living in an affluent area where the sun shines every day under a gorgeous rainbow. We live in the mist, we're a gray zone where there is no law to protect the innocent," Dave tried to explain. "This isn't my opinion since I came asking for your help, but it's the feeling of the majority of the people here. Yesterday, a teenage girl was a victim of a rape attempt. If it weren't for the fact that I was casually passing by and gave her the chance to leave, her life would be ruined. I seriously doubt she reported the case to the police. People here know that if they ask your help, they might get killed in revenge, so perhaps it's better to stay safe and alive."

Officer Orwell knew the situation of those degraded neighborhoods very well.

He didn't agree with the decision of the victims to leave crimes unreported, but on the other hand, he was aware of the flaws in the justice system. "I'll try to talk to them, perhaps, after having searched the apartment. I might also pretend to move here incognito and see what I can obtain from the people around here. But now, I need to seize the place as a potential crime scene. Show me the office of the superintendent."

"Sure, come with me; his office is in the basement." They walked downstairs without exchanging another word, but Dave felt grateful for the attention received from the Officer of the Detective Bureau.

Perhaps the other tenants should have more faith in the police. They had their flaws, but don't we all? "Here is Mr. Jones' office..." he pointed with his finger at a door as they reached the basement.

Before knocking at the door, Officer Orwell dismissed Dave. From that moment on, the investigation would become confidential material, and no one had access to that kind of information. "Thank you, for now. I think I got enough data to start looking for Ms. Burroughs. If I have any news to share, or if I need to ask more questions, I'll be in touch with you. But now, I'll ask you to return to your business and wait for my call."

Dave wasn't sure he wanted to leave right at that moment. He wished to know if she'd left any address or telephone number, but he also understood that confidentiality was a necessity.

After all, he was sure that once there was any news, he'd be the first one to receive it. "Of course," Dave whispered in a defeated tone, pushing his hands in his pockets. "I'll be waiting for your call."

As soon as he was alone in front of Mr. Jones' office, Officer Orwell knocked at the door, hoping to find someone inside.

"Yes," the calm voice of Mr. Jones replied from the room.

"Good afternoon, Mr. Jones, I'm Officer Kane Orwell from the Detective Bureau. May I steal some of your time to answer a couple of questions?" He introduced himself showing his badge.

Mr. Jones was not expecting that visit.

In his long career as superintendent of that building, not once had a detective come inside his office.

Not because crime wasn't common, but because for each murder, a killer was found amongst the list of the usual suspects well-known by the police. He stood a bit embarrassed, as the place was not well-ordered.

"What can I do for you, Officer?" he asked sheepishly.

"I would like some information about one of the former tenants of this building. I'm looking for every detail you can give me about Ms. Gloria Burroughs, who lived in number 35," Kane asked kindly.

"You're not the first one who came to ask me about that girl. Mr. Stanford also came asking about her. He found the place where she lived open and empty. I told him that she left in a hurry and gave me back the keys of the apartment," he recalled.

"Did you give them to the owner?" Kane wondered, suspecting something was going on, as the door was still open. Mr. Jones scratched his head, trying to recall what happened to the keys.

"After having informed him, I left them in the mailbox locker, as we used to do here. I don't know whether he got them, or if they're still there. Why?"

"Because I went there, and the apartment's door was open. Are you aware of this detail?" Open-mouthed, Mr. Jones remained speechless.

He didn't check the door, as he was supposed to do, and although the apartment was completely empty, without anything worth stealing, he was responsible for checking its status after Gloria returned the keys.

With his heartbeat racing in his chest for the shame and fear of the consequences, he couldn't justify his negligence. "No, I-I admit not having double-checked this detail." His voice trembled.

"Can you show me the mailbox locker of the owner of the apartment?" The situation became fascinating as the smallest pieces of the puzzle appeared on the table.

Unfortunately, none of them fit together. Yet, Mr. Jones stood from his chair, grabbed the spare keys to the mailbox of the owner of number 35, and guided Kane there. "Here is number 35," he murmured with a lower tone of voice as he jerked the key to open the locker.

With a relieved sigh, he acknowledged that the key had already been taken, but either the owner checked the conditions of the apartment and forgot to lock the door, or he didn't bother to look at it to check that everything was in order and no damage had been done to the property.

"Hmm, that's interesting," Kane mumbled. "You'd better lock the door, but I'll also need a copy of the key. The place is under investigation as a potential crime scene. Did she leave any address or contact information?"

"No, she didn't. I asked her, but she didn't know where she was going," Mr. Jones explained.

"You said she was in a hurry; do you recall whether she looked worried or scared?" Kane pursued, determined to fit those puzzle pieces he'd found.

"Hmm... I didn't pay attention to her. I received the keys, I let her undersign the resignation from the rental contract, and she left. But perhaps she was in a hurry to solve the bureaucratic stuff and leave as soon as possible." Mr. Jones shrugged.

"Can you give me the name and address of the owner of the apartment? I'll need to ask him or her some questions."

Mr. Jones shook his head. "Of course, I'll fetch the information for you."

When they returned to the office, Mr. Jones turned to one drawer where he kept all the accountancy books together with the records of the owners and tenants of every single apartment in that building.

"Here it is," he laid a big register on the table. "I don't trust any technology; these books remain here even when there is a blackout or some problems with the satellites."

Kane smiled but didn't reply; in his mind, he began to formulate all the possible reasons for a girl to run away, mainly when she had a friend like Dave to whom she could ask for help.

"You should also have a copy of the rental agreement and of her ID or social security card..." Kane questioned, as he started to look for the owner of number 35. Looking around himself, scanning the shelves, he grimaced.

"Yes, I guess so," Mr. Jones tried to recall where the book was. "Here it must be." Mr. Jones took a book from a shelf and browsed the pages until he found what he was looking for. "Here is the copy of her ID and the form she filled out when she moved in," he cheered victoriously.

"I'll need it," Kane asked, still browsing the previous register.

"You can take the whole file. Since she's no longer living here, her documents aren't needed. Let me ask you something, do you think something has happened to her?"

"I'm afraid that the way she left, without saying goodbye and in such a hurry, it doesn't give many other possibilities. A person doesn't leave from today to tomorrow if there isn't a real menace to his or her life. Something frightened her, and I'm going to find out what it was before it finds her." *And hopefully, she's still safely out of the grasp of the threat she escaped from*, Kane thought.

"That would be terrible. Despite what the other tenants here said, she was one of the few who never gave any problems, but you know better than me that having a prostitute who receives her customers in her apartment isn't something people wish as a neighbor," Mr. Jones commented.

"Was her business a source of disturbance?" Kane wondered as he collected the documents he needed to be examined later.

"To be honest, no. Not a noise ever came either from her apartment or from any of the visitors she had. She was discreet."

"Do you think she had been threatened by people living in this building?"

"Those who considered her an immoral presence would never resort to violent acts. Then, there are those who live on the other side of the law, and they're a threat to everyone. She might have been scared by them and thought it safer to move away. Most of the people here, although they're threatened, they cannot leave because of their jobs and families," Mr. Jones explained.

When Kane thought he had collected enough data from the superintendent, he left and started to put the few pieces of that puzzle together.

The sun had set for a long time, and the streets brightened up with the traffic lights. Regardless of this, he was intrigued by the case, and instead of driving back home, he took the direction to his office.

There he could file all the data and gather more information from the citizen's database.

"Here we are, Ms. Burroughs," Kane yawned. "It seems like I will continue looking for you tomorrow, and I'll also need to keep an eye on what is happening in that neighborhood. Apparently we neglected it quite too much and it's full of interesting people."

He stood from his desk and glanced at the clock. "It's almost midnight. I should be asleep. I have to be awake in seven hours." With a lazy movement, he grabbed his coat.

In his career, he'd seen many cases. Some were promptly solved; others remained to curse his nightmares.

Nevertheless, he couldn't explain why this case felt so essential and intrigued him that much. Perhaps it's the fact that there are so many players in this case that need a careful and precise classification.

Each of them might be the potential stalker, killer, kidnapper, abusive friendship. *I'll need some time to categorize them,* Kane thought as he parked his car in the parking lot of the building where his apartment was.

CHAPTER 6

The morning after, Kane reached the Police Department later than usual.

Waking up and leaving the comfort of his bed was one of the most demanding tasks he'd ever had to accomplish in his whole life.

Although he was intrigued by the case he started to investigate, the bed offered better arguments over everything else.

It wasn't a fair battle between two titans, the comfort and the softness of the bed, versus his sense of duty.

The latter came out victorious, even though severely wounded, to which only the most robust coffee he could brew had any healing power.

He reached his computer and started to go through what he'd done the night before, hoping to get brighter ideas about what happened to Gloria.

"According to the last records, she came to the building a few months ago." He began to recap the information he'd obtained so far. "Before, she lived her life moving from place-to-place, year after year, probably because of the nature of her job.

"Nevertheless, it seemed like nobody ever filed a missing person's report on her, and her moves seemed to be planned with some advance notice. This, at least, according to the records of the moving companies she'd hired. Her second to the last residence had been an exception to this rule.

"On that occasion, she moved away to a furnished apartment, as stated on the lease she'd undersigned," Kane mumbled, going through all the information he'd collected the previous day. "I'm wondering whether the mysterious *'Humphrey Bogart,'* as Mr. Stanford called him, had something to do with all the times she moved away. I think I'll pay a visit to those people who still live there."

He grabbed his coat and left the office, determined to reach her former residence. Getting inside the car, he held his breath for a second. "It will take half a day to arrive there. I hope it will be worth the trip, or I might lose precious time. Also, I should question those who are living in the same building about the same man. If I can manage, I might do this either this evening or tomorrow."

That early afternoon, he reached the address he got from the citizen register, and after parking the car, he took some time to explore the surroundings.

The neighborhood appeared to be better than the latest one, but his judgment was only founded on appearances, and they were, most of the time, deceiving.

He wasn't familiar with the place, but something told him things would have changed quite soon. The spaces on the first floor of the building were rented by shops.

He knew those were the best starting point to ask questions about the habits of the people living in the neighborhood. In particular, they could offer valuable information about the tenants of the apartments.

He went inside a clothing shop. With a fast glance at the disposition of the stands, he spotted a girl arranging the clothes on the hangers.

"Excuse me, may I ask you a few questions?" he asked, showing his badge.

The girl furrowed her brows and withdrew a couple of steps. "I only work here."

"Relax, I'm not investigating any irregularity of this shop," Kane assured, keeping a calm tone of voice. "Have you ever seen this person?" he took a copy of the picture of Gloria's ID from his pocket and showed it to her.

Displaying a shy smile, she reached for the paper with still shaky hands and observed it. Investigating the picture like she was trying to recall whether she had seen Gloria or not, she tilted her head before handing the sheet back to Kane. "The face isn't new to me. I might have seen her around, but not recently."

"Did she ever come inside this shop, perhaps to buy some clothes or to browse?" Kane insisted, gently folding the paper and placing it in a pocket of his jacket.

"I can't say..." She brought her right hand to cover her mouth. "I believe I've seen her somewhere, but I can't recall where. I guess it has been quite some time."

"Perhaps a few months ago? Last summer in a pub, or walking the streets, or coming inside this building where she lived?" Kane pursued, trying to make her remember something.

She closed her eyes, shifting her hand to her temples to force her memory to recall something she archived already. "Oh, sure."

She patted a hand against her forehead, opening her eyes as if struck by lightning. "I saw her coming and leaving from that door. I guess she lived in this same building because I could see her every day. Then, she didn't show up. Now I remember her because I loved the color of her hair; it was so shiny."

"Perhaps she moved away. One other question, and then I promise I'll let you work in peace," Kane promised, displaying his best smile.

"Do you live far from here?" "Not really." She blushed at his smile. "A few blocks away, why?"

"Because I'm wondering if your attention was attracted by someone hanging around here."

"Well, this is the kind of neighborhood where you can find all sorts of people, and it all depends on what you mean by strange," she giggled.

"I understand, but perhaps a person who doesn't fit with the environment, someone who caught your attention in a particular way?" He wanted to know whether the same one described by Dave was also seen there.

The girl remained silent to think about it for a moment, not sure she understood what he meant by it.

She tried to focus on all the people she'd seen recently who could be considered too ordinary to fit that colorful environment. "Let me think. Perhaps there is one person who fits the description, but I haven't seen him either, at least for a couple of months," she struggled to recall. "I haven't seen him in the face, but he came here around every evening, and he wore a light brown coat with a fedora hat. You know, there aren't many people wearing those kinds of hats nowadays. Perhaps he was an elderly man, as I cannot imagine a youngster dressing up in such an old-fashioned style."

Glancing at her through narrowed eyelids, he stiffened his lips. "A man with a fedora hat, you say? That's interesting, and do you know whether he entered one of those buildings or he just passed by?"

"No, I can't say so. When I'm working, I only have the time to give a fast glance outside, when something strange catches my attention. I'm not going to follow every move," she giggled, amused, turning her face to the windows.

"That will be all. Thank you for your time and have a nice day." Kane turned his back to her and strode toward the exit, waving his hand.

"You're welcome. I hope you find whoever you're looking for," she watched him walk away.

"I hope so too," he whispered, leaving the shop. Kane was confident he was on the right path, as it seemed wherever Gloria went, the mysterious Humphrey Bogart appeared. "I wonder whether the people living here could give me some more information about it."

He stopped at the front door of the building where Gloria used to live before.

Perhaps there was a chance to talk to the superintendent, who generally holds most of the knowledge about what's going on in the building he works in.

Scanning the doorbells, he looked for that of the superintendent, and when he found it, he pressed the button.

"Who's there?" asked a steady, menacing voice from the video intercom.

"Ehm, good afternoon, this is Officer Orwell. May I come inside and ask some questions?" Kane asked, taken aback by her almost angry inflection.

"Can you show me the badge?" Her tone sounded even more threatening, as if this was a common trick used by small criminals to access and intrude on other people's property. "Sure," he mumbled placing the badge in front of the camera.

"When you come inside, turn on the left at the end of the corridor. I'll open the door for you." Her voice changed to a calmer and amiable tone, making him doubt she was the same person.

A light buzz informed him the door was open, granting him access to the building.

"Good afternoon, Officer," a lady in her forties greeted him with a bright smile on her face. "I hope your visit hasn't anything to do with the administration of this condo. We care about running the business as smoothly as possible."

"No, don't you worry. To be honest, I came here to ask a few questions about a former tenant. Do you remember this girl?" Kane showed her the picture of Gloria's ID.

"I do recall her." She nodded. "She lived here for about one year, and then decided to move away. Such a lovely girl, always happy with a bright smile on her face. One of the few who never gave me any kind of problems. You know, sometimes, in particular, young people tend to be noisy, listening to loud music until late, having parties... you name it. She was, instead, discreet and quiet."

"Do you have any idea where she worked?"

"No, all I know is she had a job to sustain herself, as she used to leave the apartment at the same time every morning and returned about the same time in the afternoon. Of course, it can also be that she studied, or she went to the library every day, but since she never missed a payment for the rent, I believe she was going to work," the superintendent lifted his shoulders. "Did anything happen to her?"

"I hope not, and this is what I'm trying to find out. Do you recall if she had any visitors?"

"Sir, I do mind my own business. I take care of the administration of the building, and if the tenants are having visitors or not, this is none of my business," she tightened her features.

"I didn't mean to doubt your discretion, only if you noticed anyone who used to visit her with a certain regularity, almost daily?" Kane wondered. "Let me reformulate the question: Did you notice any unusual visitor who entered the door? Administrating the building means also taking care of the security and knowing who is coming in and out, which doesn't mean being nosy."

She sighed. "This is something you should ask the surveillance company. Cameras are installed on every floor, as I cannot check every person who is allowed in by every single tenant. If they open the door, it means they trust the visitor. This isn't a prison, and I'm not a guardian."

"You're right. I'm sorry if I've been rude with my questions. Did the girl, Gloria, leave any address or telephone number when she left?" he wondered.

"No, she intended to move away, and within a week the apartment became, once again, vacant."

"Can you tell me where she lived?"

"Hold on, I need to check it," she walked back to the desk to scroll on her database.

"Here, she lived on the third floor, at number 15."

"Is the place still vacant?"

"No, it was rented once again after one week since her departure. This isn't a popular and fancy area, but it's cheap, which makes it more than desired." Kane nodded thoughtfully.

"Can you give me the address of the firm that provides the security services to this building? I think I might need the recordings of the surveillance cameras."

"Of course, I can give you their business card here, where you might find all the contact information you might need. But won't you need a warrant to obtain the recordings?"

"Not necessarily. I'll first try to see whether they're willing to share the footage with me." He winked. "I think for now it's all I need. Thank you very much for your time and cooperation, and I wish you a pleasant evening."

"It's my pleasure, and I hope you find what you're looking for, Officer," she opened the door for him.

He inspected the business card he received and glanced around to spot any surveillance cameras.

Checking the position of the cameras on every floor gave him an idea of what to expect from them.

Retracing his steps, he started to climb the stairs until the second floor. *I believe the same camera system has been installed on every level,* he considered.

Reaching the second floor, he raised his gaze to the ceiling and observed where the cameras were pointed.

Hmm... their position seems to indicate that there is a fair chance to get a precise idea about every visitor she had, and also about her habits. This might be an invaluable piece of information, and it's a pity that the same security system wasn't installed in the last building; that would have been even better, he started to consider, as he made a small sketch about the position of the cameras in his agenda book. *Now I only need to call them, and eventually, fix an appointment.*

The man who answered the phone, introducing himself as the info desk of the security firm, seemed to be a reasonable man. His voice sounded calm and kind.

When Kane introduced himself and the purpose of his call, there wasn't any hesitation, and he was invited to visit them at their headquarters a few miles away from where he called from.

As he reached the building, Kane was received by the area manager, Mr. Clayton. "Good afternoon, Officer Orwell. You're in luck, as I'm on my way to leave for a two-week holiday," Mr. Clayton greeted, inviting Kane to take a seat on the chair in front of his desk.

Kane looked around the room, and it didn't take much time to realize how security is a vital issue for many people, making the business one of the most profitable.

The windows of the office, reaching the ceiling and taking the whole space of the outer walls, had a stunning view over the rest of the city.

The furniture, although simple, was of the finest quality.

"As my assistant told me, you're here to ask to view the footage recorded in one of the buildings downtown. Could you be more specific about it?" Mr. Clayton asked kindly.

"Of course, I need the recording of the third floor of the building on Roosevelt Avenue 110, particularly the camera pointed at the apartment number 15. I'm in the middle of an investigation for a missing person. I need to examine the content," Kane explained, hoping to be able to get the chance to start examining the tape as soon as possible, even the same day.

I'm sorry to disturb you so late, but I hope to get permission granted for tomorrow or the following day, Kane hoped.

Mr. Clayton remained silent for a while considering what to do.

There wasn't any reason to deny the officer the content of the surveillance camera, but the working day was almost at an end, and he had to leave for the holidays.

Tomorrow morning the plane will leave, and I still need to pack my clothes. What can I do? He struggled, desperate to find a solution to fit the needs of them all.

Mr. Clayton raised his glance at him. "The problem is there won't be any useful time today. It's five o'clock and most of my assistants have left already. What I can do for you is to leave an order to my colleague, Mrs. Jenkins, to allow you to go through the footage in the morning. Unfortunately, without a warrant I can't give you the recording, but you can come here and watch it for as long as you need it. I can arrange a room for this purpose, but this is going to be for tomorrow."

Kane felt more than satisfied with that condition.

He wasn't counting on having a copy of the footage for himself, and the chance to view the morning after was more than fine for him. "I appreciate your help, and I believe I can wait if you assure me I won't find any resistance from your assistants." Kane smiled.

"Why would they? We give security camera services for this reason, so people will feel safer about who is coming and who is leaving. Then, in case of burglary, murder or any other crime, the police will have better tools to find out who is responsible."

Kane nodded. "Fine, at what time may I come tomorrow morning?"

"Mrs. Jenkins will be here, as usual, at half past eight. You might come at that time," Mr. Clayton stood from his chair and walking to the reception area, followed by Kane. "Jack, tomorrow morning, Officer Orwell will come to review some footage we recorded. Give him full access and ask Johanna to assist him in anything he might need," Mr. Clayton addressed to the man at the desk.

"Yes, Mr. Clayton. Do you want me to prepare him a guest key card, so he can have access at any time of the day?" Jack suggested promptly.

"That's a fantastic idea, but now I need to go, or I'll be late. Explain everything to him and make sure as he leaves everything is going to be ready for tomorrow morning," Mr. Clayton said, and then he turned to face Kane. "I'm sorry to leave in such a hurry. I wish I had more time to familiarize you with the environment, but unfortunately, this is a bad time. Please, accept my apologies if I might sound rude."

"No, I understand. What's important for me is having the possibility to see the recording. I arrived unannounced. You were very kind to give me the chance to examine the footage. I appreciate your availability."

Mr. Clayton smiled. "I hope you will find useful information for your investigation. Now I need to go. I wish you a nice evening, and if in the future you might need any help, don't hesitate to contact us."

"Thank you and have a great holiday," Kane greeted as Mr. Clayton went out the door.

When he left the office of the security company, it was already dark, and a fine rain started to fall insistently.

Kane knew that returning home would be a waste of time; therefore, he decided to spend the night there, trying to find accommodations for that night. At least something better than spending the night in my car, he thought.

December was not the easiest time to find a hotel room without any reservations.

Still, he managed to find a reasonable place in a close-by bed and breakfast. "Something I'm wondering about this case is why Mr. Stanford didn't act immediately. I know it was a couple of days after she disappeared, but when this kind of thing happens, the earlier they tell us, the better outcome we can expect. I need to ask someone at the Department to seize the apartment where she was living and start to search there for any evidence. We need to get information about the owner and set up a patrol in case the strange avenger is going to show up again," he entered the room.

Grabbing his mobile phone, he emailed his supervisor, knowing this might be the best way to organize the work... "Alone, I can't take care of everything, and already now, this case starts to appear to be more complicated than it seemed in the beginning," he chuckled.

With a groan, he sat on the bed and took out the picture of Gloria, and shook his head... "Whoever you are, wherever you are, I will find you. The only thing I hope is to do it before it's too late; I'm sick and tired of finding only corpses."

Silence filled the room as he listened to the ghosts coming to haunt his nights. His expression toughened, and he stood from the bed, wondering whether he could find some sleep with all the thoughts he had in his mind.

He considered starting to write down all the information he'd gathered so far; he was sure of being on the right path, and recording his previous moves was a brilliant idea. "I'm sure this mysterious man followed her since here. Perhaps, until here, she considered him a nuisance, but when she moved away and found out he followed her, she started to fear for her life and left. Unless he could get her and cleaned the place of every trace.

"What seems strange to me is she went away in a hurry, and a person who is leaving because she fears for her life doesn't stop to clean the apartment. In this case, since she rented a furnished flat, she'd left it with open drawers, perhaps the kitchen would have not been spotless... This makes me fear either she planned her move in advance, and she left without telling anyone, or whoever took her forcibly wanted to clean the crime scene. Yet, even in this case, the fact that she returned the keys herself doesn't seem right."

He began to pace around the room, unable to find some peace. "Fuck! Nothing makes sense in this story, and besides, who is the mysterious avenger of which they're talking about?"

He sat down at the writing table and started to put things down once again. "Gloria is a prostitute; she's working, placing announcements in magazines or night clubs. She seems to be careful in choosing the customers, but one day a gentleman appears and becomes her customer. This man starts to be a bit too insistent, perhaps asking for services Gloria isn't comfortable with. For this reason, she decides to move away, believing this has solved her problem," he said, writing his notes.

"The gentleman isn't so gentle after all and searches for her, until he finds where she is, and goes to her apartment. In the beginning, he apologizes and promises he will behave, so she feels confident that nothing bad is going to happen to her. She becomes a friend with Dave, who gifted her with three of his drawings. The area is violent, but since she arrived, a mysterious avenger appears, killing some low-life criminals who terrorize the neighborhood. At the same time, the gentleman returns to be insistent... Hold it!" he raised his gaze to the window. "What if the customer has nothing to do with her disappearance? What if this avenger considers her as part of the criminal life to be eliminated?"

He shook his head. "I need more information... I need more pieces in this puzzle, and tomorrow I'll get a better picture once I go through the footage. Until then, I do not have any chance to put those pieces together, and I should try to get some sleep without thinking about it anymore. It won't help me trying to solve a case without the necessary information. It would be like asking a blind person to describe a rainbow." He started to undress, ready to go under the shower to relax a bit.

He didn't even think of going for dinner, and honestly, he wasn't yet hungry.

Every time he followed a case like that, his weight dropped drastically. That wasn't something he planned; it was his nature.

He couldn't think of eating when this meant stealing time from the investigation. "I can't wait until I retire. I promise I'll move to a deserted island where no internet or newspapers can reach me to show me how cruel people can be with each other."

CHAPTER 7

The insistent ringing of the doorbell lacerated the thin curtain of peaceful sleep, causing a loud growl to escape from Dave's mouth.

That was the first time it happened, and he wondered whether the house was burning, and he had slept through the sirens of the fire brigade.

"I'm coming..." he muttered groggily, trying not to stumble on anything on his way to reach the door.

As he unlocked the door, someone slammed it open and grabbed him.

Everything happened too fast for him to understand the dynamics, but whoever the intruder was, he seized him and forced him to face the wall.

The click of handcuffs locking on his wrists sharpened his senses enough to awaken him to the presence of two officers holding tightly to him, while two other agents searched his apartment.

It took a couple of minutes to understand who and what they were doing and what they said.

Yet, he failed to fathom what in the hell was happening.

"Mr. Dave Stanford, you're under arrest for the murder of Jonathan Braxton, Steven Chalker, and Alan McMillen," the officer who cuffed him explained.

With his heart jumping in his chest, he woke up at their accusation. "Say fucking what?" he yelled, trying to turn himself to face the policeman. "I haven't killed anyone! I haven't stood up to any bully in my whole life!" Dave added desperately. "You got the wrong man. I'm innocent, and by the way, who the heck are those people?"

The policeman smirked. "Of course, you're like all the other maniacs," he pushed him out of his apartment.

"At least let me put something on!" He wriggled violently, refusing to go out almost naked. Christmas holidays were approaching and going out in the chilly winter only in his boxer briefs wasn't something he considered appropriate.

I'm still entitled to some human rights, even if they consider me a killer. This is all Shauna's fault and all those people who think it's cool to deem me the avenger of this neighborhood! He had no clue how to escape such a mess.

The fear of being accused of Gloria's disappearance crossed his mind, as adrenaline rushed in his blood.

Officer Orwell represented his only hope in that complicated case.

He was still investigating the events, and perhaps he found enough leads to push away any suspicion from him.

The officer huffed, annoyed. "Fine, let's get you dressed, but I warn you, one false move, and we'll have another casualty," he warned, pointing his gun at him.

As Dave got his wrists freed from the cuffs, he searched for his trousers and shirt to put on, and soon after, they guided him out of his apartment to the car, ready to be brought to the Police Department for interrogation.

Out on the street, a slim group of people gathered to assist in the arrest of the person believed to be the avenger.

By their judging eyes fixed on him, following every move, he acknowledged their certainty of his guilt; they knew it, also without any proof of his involvement in any of those murders.

Overwhelmed by shame, he lowered his gaze to avoid eye contact with any of those people who knew he'd been framed by their stupid rumors.

With bitterness in his mouth, he entered the police car, hoping to leave as soon as possible.

Most likely, they asked around and my beloved neighbors confirmed they saw me at all the crime scenes, he thought. For fuck's sake, if living in the same building makes me a murderer, you can count at least a hundred more suspects to be interrogated... Why me?

Confused by the mixed feelings and thoughts swirling in his mind, his only goal was to understand why the officers believed the rumors without gathering any proof.

He tried several times to say something, to ask questions about the reason for being brought to the Police Station for interrogation about murders he hadn't committed.

Yet, he couldn't find any breath to say a word; his heart racing in his chest choked the words in his throat. He wanted to scream and cry, but he was frozen in a single moment.

Also, the officers who were with him remained silent.

He wondered whether this was something that happened regularly or if they, too, considered that arrest strange. "Why am I accused of murder?" Dave almost whispered.

None of them answered. *Did they hear me? Perchance the tone of my voice was too faint to be heard.*

Inhaling deeply to gather more air in his lungs, he repeated his question louder, hoping to receive an answer from any of them.

"Someone caught sight of you at the crime scene, and they believe you're involved in that murder," one of the officers explained, keeping his eyes on the road.

"I live in that building, like hundreds of other people. This can't make me a killer. I can't be accused of murder because I live in the same place where all those murders took place. You can't arrest a person because he lives in the same building... Why me, then?" His voice increased in tone, becoming shaky, struggling to keep his tears from falling.

The other officer, who was driving the car, decided to intervene. "It's not because of where you live, but because of what other witnesses swear to have seen."

"They're lying. Do you rely only on this as proof?" Dave wondered as they arrived at the Police Station.

"You will explain this to the detective who will conduct the interrogation," the officer helped Dave coming out of the car.

They guided him to a room supposed to be used for the questioning and asked Dave to wait.

The cuffs on his wrist were secured to the table so he couldn't leave the place. As he remained alone in the room, Dave shook his head, still failing to believe what had happened.

This must be a nightmare. Yet, if it isn't, I promise as soon as I'm released-because I WILL as, I'm innocent – I'll find another place to go. It doesn't matter whether I have to live in the worst area or neighborhood, what is important is that I'll move away from those people who thought spreading rumors that I was the avenger was a brilliant idea. Yes, maybe for them, but what about me? I'm facing going to jail for the rest of my life for crimes I've never committed. Fuck them all!

Furious, disappointed, frustrated, but most of all scared – scared to death of the unpredictability of the situation he got into – Dave grabbed his head between his hands.

Everything started with the arrival of Gloria, but why am I now thinking about Gloria? She's also missing, and nobody can tell whether she's still alive... Why me? Why me?

Holding his head tightly, tears began to fall, dripping on the table in large and heavy drops. Then the door opened, and another officer came in, and without saying anything he took a seat in front of Dave, who tried to stop crying.

"Mr. Stanford, do you know the reason why you have been arrested?" he asked, noticing Dave's emotional state.

"The officers told me I'm accused of murder, but I don't know how I got inside this story. I haven't killed anyone – not now, and neither am I thinking of doing anything similar. I lived my life in the gray area many people try to avoid, and now in the blink of an eye, I'm brought into the spotlight. Why?" Dave raised his glance at the detective who entered the room.

"After the second murder, where Mr. Braxton was killed, we received a few anonymous calls. They were all pointing at you as responsible for those murders. Of course, we do not take into consideration just that, but we decided to ask around what your neighbors think about you. Some describe you as a weird person, a solitary man without any friends. Others said you saved the life of a little girl, but they suspected you were a sort of avenger who stood to fight those rotten people who are causing only harm. So now I ask you: Who are you?" the detective asked, entwining his fingers over the desk.

"None of the people you've described. Besides, my private life is nobody's business, and whether I've friends or not, they cannot say, unless they follow me every day. Not being a social person doesn't make me a murderer, it makes me lonely, yet, I repeat, not a killer," Dave insisted, enunciating every word of the last sentence.

"Do you have any friends?" the detective asked.

"I had Gloria..." Dave mumbled.

"Your girlfriend?"

"Just a friend. She lived in one apartment on my same floor."

"She has been described as a prostitute..." Dave raised his eyes at him and glanced at him with disdain.

"What do you or any of those people know about her? She's the sweetest girl in the world, besides being the only one who could see me."

"I can see you," the detective objected, arching his eyebrow.

Tilting his head backward, Dave huffed. "Only because the circumstances force you to do so. Trust me, had you met me in the metro, on the street, or at the bar beside you, you wouldn't perceive my presence. She saw me without being forced to, maybe because she's also invisible like me."

"So, taking advantage of your invisibility, you killed those people?" Pursuing in a threatening tone, he got close enough to Dave's face to smell his fear.

"I didn't kill them, and you don't have any proof, besides the word of someone who is cowardly hiding behind an anonymous call." Dave's voice flickered, but there wasn't any doubt he'd been framed.

"Where is this girl now? Can she testify in your favor?" The detective leaned back in his chair.

"I wish she could. She left without leaving any trace. I came here to file a case for a missing person, and Detective Orwell is following it. Why don't you ask him?" Kane was perhaps his last resort, the one who could save him from an impossible situation.

"Detective Kane Orwell?" Tilting his head, the officer wondered.

"I guess so." Without saying another word, he jumped from his chair and rushed out of the room, like the Devil chased his soul.

Unaware of the circumstances, Dave started to feel hungry and thirsty, but he feared he would be without any water for a long time.

After a wait that felt like an eternity, the detective returned and uncuffed Dave's wrists.

"You're free to go," he stated, without bothering to explain the reason for his release. Dave glanced at him through narrowed eyelids and didn't move.

Regardless of the desire to run away, something didn't fit with that change of attitude, and he was almost scared to leave the place. "What do you mean I can leave? Just before you left, you were ready to slam me into prison for the rest of my life. You had no doubt about my involvement, and now I'm free."

"I called Detective Orwell. He explained to me what he'd found out so far about the disappearance of this girl. According to him, the mysterious avenger might be the same man who followed her for a couple of years. If this is true, then it's impossible for you to be the killer."

His voice returned to be calm, and the menacing tone faded away, giving space to a kind, almost apologetic intonation. "Moreover, our agents didn't find anything to connect you to the murders in your apartment. Nevertheless, I would like you to remain available, because I have the strange impression someone is interested in framing you, either as a way to misdirect the investigation or to get rid of you. We will need to keep you under surveillance to understand who this person is and why they're after you."

"Do you think someone is planning to kill me? What for?" Dave wondered.

He felt relieved for their understanding. Someone believed he had nothing to do with the murders, yet he wasn't entirely convinced about his tone. "Where is Detective Orwell?"

"He's out of town to search for this girl. He'll be back no earlier than this late evening. He will contact you tomorrow."

Dave nodded thoughtfully and stood from the chair, ready to return to his apartment, from where he hoped he could continue to live his life in the same gray anonymity he was condemned to.

Before leaving the room, he turned once again to the officer. "Did Detective Orwell tell you whether he gathered any information about Gloria's present location?"

"He will tell you everything he found out when he contacts you. Meanwhile, I suggest you continue your life as usual, without raising any suspicions about our surveillance. It would be beneficial if you would refrain from telling anyone what has happened here today and the reason why we have released you. In particular, we would appreciate it if you would keep this detail to yourself."

Dave nodded. He wasn't convinced about what the detective's words, and there was a little nagging voice, which insisted yelling they were still considering him the murderer, and they were going to follow every move he made to confirm his innocence or guilt.

Either way I feel positive. If they're going to follow me in my everyday life, they will get definitive proof of whoever is trying to frame me, he thought. *What disconcerts me is the presence of someone willing to bring me to jail to save himself. The question, in this case, is why me? Why did they choose me as a scapegoat and not any other tenant of the building? We all live there, and we might have a more or less solid alibi, yet what we all have in common is the lack of empathy for those people who had been killed.*

It was true, and everybody hoped the mysterious avenger to be a person like Dave, one of those individuals who could incarnate the ideal of the hero, the one with the kind of morals allowing him to terminate the life of someone to protect the safety of many others.

The problem is that the police don't care whether I do it for a noble cause or because I'm a monster.

The law is clear, and no one is supposed to take justice into their own hands – Dave thought, reaching the subway station to go to his office.

He called his supervisor and explained what had happened to him. He hoped he would understand and didn't get too upset about the fact that he didn't inform him about the situation.

"We had a call from the police, and they informed me of your arrest. Is there anything you need to tell me about yourself?" his supervisor wondered.

"No, they got the wrong person. I don't live in a fancy area, and there, violent crimes are daily news. After they understood I had nothing to do with them, they released me. I'm sorry, but I didn't have the time to call you and inform you about the situation I had." Dave feared the whole editorial staff knew about this incident and had drawn conclusions about it.

"I understand and if you prefer to take a day off, you're free to do so. Nobody would like to be accused unfairly," his supervisor suggested.

"No, I think I need to get to work and try to forget about this morning. I'll be there in about one hour."

"As you wish, see you soon, then."

"Of course, bye." Dave stared at the telephone in fear. He didn't know what to expect at work, but he was sure that taking a day off right away could be interpreted as an admission of guilt.

He drew a deep breath and struggled to go on with his ordinary life, and as the train went on in its route, he closed his eyes and tried to convince himself it was all a bad dream, and as soon as he got off the train, his usual gray existence would continue from the point he'd left it, just like every day.

Walking the distance between the station and the building of the newspaper his mind got clearer, and he almost forgot about what happened in the morning, and after all, why think about it or dwell on it? He was innocent and released.

However, the situation changed when he stepped into the floor where he worked.

People noticed him arriving and although they did their best to hide their curiosity, Dave could sense their questioning eyes following his every move.

He tried to ignore them and pretend nothing had happened, but their insistent gazes upon him felt like thousands of blades stabbing him with every step he took toward his office.

The door closing behind him offered him final relief from that oppressive situation, and he allowed himself to collapse on the chair as a loud moan escaped him.

He started up the computer and immersed himself in his tasks, determined to work for as long as possible, leaving after all the others.

After a few hours, he hoped his colleagues had left for the lunch break or were busy working in their own offices.

Like a thief, he sneaked out of his office, almost tiptoeing along the aisles. He hoped to reach the kitchen, where he could have at least a cup of coffee without being noticed.

The corridors and the halls were almost empty, and the sensation of loneliness gave him a sort of comfortable feeling of not having to justify himself in front of anyone else but himself.

However, something he had not expected was everybody being gathered in the kitchen, and as soon as he entered, a grave silence fell among those present.

Walking silently to the coffee machine, acting as if he didn't notice it, he started to prepare himself a coffee.

Yet that was not going to happen. He could not fool himself by pretending things hadn't changed from the usual when everybody followed every single move he made.

With an annoyed glance he turned to face them. "What's wrong?"

Joseph came out of the crowd. "What's wrong, you're asking?" he sneered with his usual cockiness.

"Yes, why in this world are you all staring at me like I'm a sort of strange animal? Until yesterday, you ignored me and didn't recall my name. Today, like a charm, I'm on everyone's mouth, and it seems like I regained my visibility. Although, it's not in the way I'd hoped for all these years. So, to answer your question, yes, I'm indeed wondering what's going on with you." Dave's tone had never been so confident.

He surprised himself too, but perhaps, after all these years of abuse he was too tired to remain silent.

Joseph shook his head. "I don't know where you come from or what you're used to, but in a civilized world a person arrested for murder doesn't have any right to ask other people 'what's wrong.'"

"Then I should remind you what the job of a journalist is all about. Your job includes giving detailed information about the facts without inserting your opinion. Indeed, I've been arrested because I was suspected of the murders in my neighborhood, but they released me because my arrest was a misunderstanding, and I've nothing to do with those crimes. I got out because he realized they got the wrong man, an innocent man, and they will continue with the investigation," Dave challenged.

"We didn't get the same impression," Joseph pursued.

"A real journalist doesn't base his knowledge on impressions, but on facts. How easy you forget about the basis of your job; perhaps you should refresh your professional skills." Dave didn't know how he got the guts to face Joseph that way, but he started to feel sick and tired of his attitude, and he needed to tell everybody he wasn't a killer.

"And what the fuck would a little shit like you know about the work of a journalist?" Joseph pushed him against the wall.

"At least more than you," intervened Alan, who covered the politics section of the newspaper. "He's right, the police released him because they found him innocent, so you should leave him alone, and so should you all, and stop judging everybody."

Goggling at Alan, he was left speechless. *And that is indeed the news of the day; not only is there someone who knows my name, but he's defending me from the most popular Mr. Fantastic,* he thought.

Joseph's expression became livid, but he struggled to keep his usual poker face. "Yes, you keep taking the side of this despicable criminal," he left the room.

All the others followed him and left Dave and Alan alone in the kitchen. "Thanks," mumbled Dave. "You didn't have to. Now they will all hate you for defending me."

Alan smiled and patted Dave's shoulder. "There isn't a greater pleasure than putting his fat head back in line. He's a good journalist and generally does an amazing job. Unfortunately, he likes to tease those who appear a little insecure. You offered him the best chance to show off; though, when you faced him, he might have not appreciated it."

"Thanks, but I think I annoyed him a little too much, and the rest of the team like him more than they like me." Dave took out the frustration he'd accumulated during his entire life.

"He'll get over it. Stay away from him for the next couple of days, and he will be back to normal, ignoring you like he always did." Alan walked away from the kitchen.

As he remained alone, he started to consider the way his life had turned upside down since Gloria came. "She came and transformed my life, but although she left, instead of returning to the usual routine, my whole existence changed radically. I'm wondering whether this will ever change, and I'll get back to my comfortable anonymity," Dave almost whispered to himself waiting for his coffee from the machine.

He returned to his office determined to stay away from everybody's sight for the whole week, like Alan suggested. "Thinking about him, I wonder why he stood up to defend me, in this place where everything seems to revolve around Joseph.

Sometimes he behaves like he owns this place," he said aloud as he continued his work.

Dave shook his head, trying to cast away all the thoughts from his mind, to get back his focus without worrying about his personal issues.

At least at work, he wished to forget everything that had happened in the past few months; he wanted to return to the times before he met Gloria and fell in love with her. *What am I thinking? I'm not in love with her*, he thought.

He remained in the office far after his regular working hours; he wanted to be the last to leave the place so as to avoid having any contact with the rest of the staff.

Reaching the exit of the building, his telephone started to ring – something he needed to get used to, as generally, it was as silent as a tomb.

"Hello," Dave answered.

"Good evening, Mr. Stanford, this is Detective Orwell. Do you have a moment to talk?"

"Of course. I just got out of work, and I'm walking to the subway station. Did you find out anything about Gloria?" Dave wondered.

"I went to check the place where she lived before she moved into the apartment close to yours," he started to explain. "By a stroke of luck, they had a surveillance camera system installed, and I could see the mysterious guy you called Humphrey Bogart visited her there as well. I can't tell the reason for his visit, whether for sexual services or something else. What's strange is everybody said she worked somewhere, but they didn't know where. Did she ever tell you anything about her life?"

"Well, I don't know what to say. She told me she chose prostitution as a way of living and this caused her to break up with her family. I suppose we should search for them, to understand whether she started to prostitute herself after she moved away from the previous place. Did she lie to me, or did she rent another apartment to run her prostitution business?" Dave wondered.

"However, we couldn't find much time to talk; our working schedules didn't match up in order to grow a more solid relationship."

"Did you ever have sex with her?"

"No, I considered her a friend. Although I found her attractive, I preferred to keep her as something I never had in my life, a friendly presence. You have no idea what it means to be invisible and ignored, but for me it was enough having someone who noticed me and wanted to be friendly. I wished we could share more time together, but... Oh, well... this is my life."

"I see," Kane mumbled. "I heard you had trouble with one of our detectives," he chuckled.

"That was the least of what happened this morning. The news of my arrest with the suspicion of murder didn't help me at work. In the beginning, I was depressed about how the other people in my workplace were ignoring me. Today, when everybody knew about the charges against me, it felt like being condemned for the assassination of those people. I don't know how I can manage to keep working there, after what happened," Dave complained.

"I'm sorry, it must be a difficult situation for you," Kane apologized.

"It's not your fault. I'm wondering why I got accused. I mean, you can find at least one hundred people who had a valid reason to kill those criminals. Thinking about the parents of those girls who had been raped or harassed, those who had children like Johnny, attracted to the criminal side, those who slipped into the use of drugs. I'm the one who is least interested in revenge against those guys. I've never been connected or harmed by any of their illegal activities. So, once again, why accuse me?" Dave wondered, still failing to believe it wasn't a nightmare.

Kane sighed. "You're right, there were indeed many others with a better reason to kill those people, starting from a member of a rival gang.

"We received a few anonymous calls indicating you as responsible for the murders. Of course, we don't give credit to every call we receive, particularly when dealing with a brutal crime like multiple murders. However, we had the duty to investigate that lead, and they had to listen to the testimony of people who live in the neighborhood." Kane grabbed a pen and started tapping on the surface of his desk. "Although they couldn't be sure, in their opinion you were the guy who is behind those murders. They considered you as a sort of avenger. Others claimed having seen you coming from the crime scene. You understand this represents a valid reason for our officers to bring you in for an interrogation."

"So, do you mean I have been watched by the police for the last few days?" Dave widened his eyes. "If so, how couldn't they grasp that it wasn't me who was the killer?"

Kane placed the pen back on the desk, glancing around. "Shauna, the girl you saved from those two thugs, recalled you yelling at them to leave her alone, and as they saw you, they ran away as if you were a ghost. Admittedly, those guys are not easily impressed by anyone."

"It surprised me as well, believe me. Instinctively, I yelled at them, being aware they might have let her go with the sole purpose of killing me instead," Dave recalled, stepping inside the train. "When they ran away terrified, I couldn't understand it. In the beginning, I thought there was someone behind me who scared them, but after they left, I focused on helping Shauna to return home. She admitted there were rumors about my involvement in the murders; she talked about an avenger, and I tried my best to make her understand it wasn't me, and they were all making a dangerous mistake. She asked me to pretend to be him because they needed someone to believe in."

Dave took a small pause and realized everything started with a simple rumor, which gave him more problems than honor. "I tried to explain to her the reason why I wouldn't pretend to be him was because of the legal repercussions, and I hoped she'd understand. However, you know how kids are, and I'm afraid she disregarded my request."

"Now everything is becoming clear, at least concerning your involvement in the case. I'll make sure this won't give you any more trouble in your life. But I believe this avenger is a figure connected to Gloria and that Humphrey Bogart. There are many pieces of this puzzle, which don't seem to fit with each other, and I'm afraid you found yourself in the middle of an intricate case," Kane raised his eyebrows.

"My usual luck, I guess," Dave stared at his hand.

"Perhaps, for once it can come in useful to us, one day. At least when it comes to finding Gloria."

"I hope so," Dave sighed walking to his apartment. "Please keep me informed about the progress of the investigation."

"Of course. One more thing, though," Kane he grabbed the pen from the desk once again and turned it around his fingers. "Could you give me the message Gloria put on your mailbox? I need to examine it closely, to see whether at the laboratory they can find anything that can give us any extra clues."

"Sure, there isn't any problem with it. Will you come to get it, or should I bring it to the Police Department?"

"If you could come tomorrow after work, we could also talk about it," Kane suggested.

Dave cringed. "I'm not feeling too confident about being there, but I'll try to overcome my feelings and reach the Police Department. I should be there at about half past four, considering the traffic at that time. I hope it won't be too late for you."

"No, it will be a good time, and perhaps there's something more I can tell you about the outcome of my search." Kane stood from his desk.

"Perfect, see you tomorrow, then."

"Sure, and have a good evening." Kane smiled.

"Thanks, and same to you." Dave hung up the conversation, glancing around as he entered his apartment. Finally, he felt safe from all the craziness of the day.

He thought about everything from the time the police irrupted in his house, cuffing and arresting him for the murder of Spike and the others, to the incident at work and all the stress he'd accumulated during that period.

He needed a vacation, but regardless of the overtime and holidays, he couldn't see the chance coming in the near future.

With a grunt, he collapsed on the couch and closed his eyes, trying to think about nothing at all, clearing his mind from all the thoughts.

After a few hours, he woke up to realize he'd fallen asleep. He glanced at the clock. "Fuck, it's half past ten in the evening. This is about the time I think about going to bed, and I haven't even had my dinner yet." Dave stood and stretched his body. "Perhaps I can eat something small, like a sandwich, browse what's on the TV, and go to sleep a bit later."

It seemed to be a brilliant idea, mainly because he knew he wouldn't be able to fall asleep after he'd been napping on the couch for at least four hours.

However, munching at his sandwich, he wondered whether it wasn't perhaps better to draw something.

That mystery inspired him, suggesting him to create a new superhero or story. His creative inspiration was running at high octane, so he took out his sketchbook, and chewing the last bit of food, he started to sketch something triggered by the recent events.

Perhaps the idea of an avenger who is going to seek revenge for the crimes against innocent people isn't entirely wrong, Dave considered, amused. I don't deny it.

I would love to be a sort of superhero, something like Superman, who behind the apparent facade of a shy and clumsy, nerdy person, hides a brave and strong fighter, who is going to reach where the inefficient police can't.

As he thought about the character he wanted to create, he drew someone who would resemble him.

He's a man who arrives and disappears with the fog. He will be the hero who comes and punishes the most horrific crimes without his victims acknowledging him arriving. He's swift and acts as a shadow...

His hand moved fast and created a superhero coming from the mist: "The man from the mist," he said observing his character.

Something similar to the sketch he gave to Gloria. The resemblance between him and the man was striking, and without thinking about it, he dressed him in a long coat and a fedora hat.

It was like mixing him and the Humphrey Bogart man who, perhaps, kidnapped Gloria. "Well, no. My hero is going to find out where Gloria is and will save her unless she has to save him. If we're talking about me as a superhero, then we need to put into perspective the fact that he will find out where she's been kept prisoner, but since he's quite clumsy, he'll need her help to reach safety."

He laughed. "This might sound a bit like those parodies of action movies, and my hero isn't really a hero. He's more a wannabe."

Observing the drawing, he shook his head. "NO! This hero is not a wannabe, and he can be dangerous, but never to those who need protection. Perhaps, he might appear like the guy next door, who can become quite threatening when provoked by injustice and crime."

Grabbing another sheet, he drew his 'Man from the Mist.' He liked the idea; he loved the fact of being protected and carried by the fog.

He stood from the chair and went to his closet. There on the upper part, an old suitcase rested.

It was full of memories; among those things he'd conserved were items from his parents' house after they died.

He barely remembered how he came into possession of that suitcase, but that evening he knew it held something inside which could help him.

With a careful and gentle touch, he opened it and grabbed an old black coat and a matching fedora hat. He wore it and admired his image in the mirror.

Indeed, he looked like his new superhero.

CHAPTER 8

The alarm clock mercilessly ringing reminded him of going to sleep earlier instead of getting excited about his new character.

At no time in his life had waking up been more painful than that morning.

Nevertheless, sketching helped him to discharge some stress, and Morpheus held him in his arms granting him a deep sleep, so he still considered it a win.

Stretching his body caused a loud groan coming from his mouth, and despite the tiredness, a smile arched his lips upward.

He was supposed to see Detective Orwell in the afternoon, who hopefully could give some positive news.

Of course, he didn't expect him to hand him a closed case with Gloria's new address and the reassurance of her well-being.

All he hoped was to obtain, at least, some information about her possible location or any proof of life. He took his time to eat his breakfast and, unhurried, enjoyed the fair winter weather as he strode to his work.

Not even the incident of the previous day seemed to be of any concern. The newborn superhero he sketched took over his shy and gray life, turning it into a brilliant diamond.

He didn't fear the judgment of his workmates, and particularly he didn't dread Joseph, who was nothing else but a fat-headed jerk, and as if he gained some superpowers, he was immune to his abuses.

Nonetheless, as it happens to every superhero, his superhuman abilities faded away as he stepped inside the lobby and started to walk toward his office.

That place was like kryptonite for him, restricting his powers, forcing him, step after step, to return to his gray, shy self.

He sighed and, recalling the advice of Alan, he strode without even thinking of stopping by the kitchen for a coffee.

Before having it, he wanted to start up with his work, organizing his tasks for the day, creating a precise schedule.

Like for many people, his life was composed of small, comfortable routines: coming into the office, starting the computer, checking the workload, arranging priorities, and a list of the editing to be done, from the most urgent to those which could wait.

Once everything was set up with his working schedule, with a relieved sense of accomplishment, he would go and enjoy his morning coffee.

By then, he also knew the kitchen should be almost empty. Of course, there wasn't any rule to that statement, and as it happened the previous day, he might meet the whole team crammed into that small room.

He inhaled deeply and sauntered to the kitchen, praying for it to be either empty or almost. His hopes and prayers were granted, as indeed only one person indulged there to read the newspaper.

Unfortunately, not the one he hoped to meet alone: Joseph.

Holding his breath, he kept walking, pretending nothing had ever happened, and like every time, without saying a word, he walked to the coffee machine. His heartbeat jumped to a crazy pace in the matter of a millisecond.

He was almost sure he would have passed out if it continued that way, the only consolation being that Joseph also pretended he never saw him coming in, although the tension between the two could be sensed like an invisible bundle of electrified wires.

Why can't I be like my hero, face people and stand my ground? Why do I shake like a leaf every time I find myself with someone in the same room? Dave clenched his fists.

Joseph followed Dave out of the corner of his eye as he walked to the coffee machine. He sensed Dave's discomfort.

Although he considered his presence quite annoying, he decided to refrain from teasing him with all those words swirling in his mind.

I don't need to state the obvious, which is his inferiority – Joseph thought – *sometimes it's better to let things go, it's not even worth the effort. Whether he's involved in the murders or not, he will always be an insignificant nullity. Perhaps the chief will decide to fire him and hire someone with a bit more character.*

Joseph's thoughts were so loud, and without even speaking them aloud, Dave heard them. Although he didn't like them, he preferred to remain in the background of Joseph's ego.

Things can escalate to a problematic level, and besides, I lived my working life in the shadow of the whole editorial team, I can go on forever in this comfortable invisibility.

When his coffee was ready, Dave walked away, feeling confident at having left the worst behind him. *Perhaps I underestimated Joseph, and after all he can be a reasonable person who can understand where to draw the line. I hope there won't be any other murders connected to the same mysterious man... Well, to be honest, I wish there wouldn't be any murders at all, our neighborhood doesn't need trouble. Already the fact of living in a cheap area, forgotten by any development plans, is hard. If we add the high crime rate, the situation can become unbearable,* Dave thought entering the lobby.

For the first time in his career, he glanced around and observed something he never hoped for. The stares of everybody directed at him gave the sensation of being naked in front of the crowd.

Their eyes judging without knowing him hit him like the slashing of razor blades on his bare skin, reaching his soul.

Being released by the police and having all the charges dropped didn't help him. They were all convinced he was the mysterious assassin; a psychopath, shy and defenseless during the day at work, who transformed during the night into a ruthless murderer.

Knowing those victims were confirmed criminals, drug dealers, rapists, and whatever else didn't ease the cruelty of their judgment.

Dave couldn't fathom whether they always looked at him in such a way. He never even dared to raise his gaze and get a glimpse of what surrounded him.

It was safer to mind his own business, doing his job the best he could, and leave at the end of the day to return to his personal life.

As they caught his wondering glance, they all returned to their own matters, pretending nothing happened.

With his heart broken, he limped carelessly to his office, and slowly, without making any noise, he closed his door, ensuring it would remain so. It was like sealing himself into an isolated part of the world, with the computer the only connection to reality.

He tried to focus on his work, without thinking about anything else but the texts he needed to edit. "That's the most important thing now. I don't care what they think about me or not. What is essential now is to produce a flawless text ready for the next edition," Dave whispered starting to go through the first document.

Suddenly, as he began reading it through, he realized the reason for the stares he received. It was a piece of news about the investigations regarding the murders he was accused of.

According to the statement released by the police "...a few suspects were arrested and although some of them were discharged for lack of evidence, they might be inquired again in the future..."

Evidently, the police didn't yet close the case of Dave's responsibility, and with his comment he could still be considered the murderer, or one of them. "Why didn't they tell me this when they released me?" He stood from his chair and walked to the window.

The roads were as busy as usual, and people hurried about on their errands. "Did they free me, assuring me they crossed-out my name from the list of suspects, only to follow every single move I make? Did they install cameras and recording devices in my apartment?" He tried to see whether he could spot a police car waiting outside of the building.

He then recalled having taken out the old coat, which belonged to his grandfather, and fear welled from the innermost part of his soul.

Since they were looking for a man with a coat and a fedora hat, he could be arrested, and perhaps they were expecting him at home. "Fuck! I'm supposed to meet Detective Orwell at the Police Department today. What if they're waiting to arrest me?"

Fear turned to panic, and his hands trembled at the certainty that in one way or another that coat would get him into serious trouble.

He wondered if it was better to go to the Police Department and see what happened. *I don't have any place to hide; they will find me if they're looking for me,* he thought. *My only hope is Detective Orwell to prove that since the Humphrey Bogart guy was following Gloria since before she moved to town, he can also be connected to those murders. After all, it's not a crime to own a coat and a fedora. For sure, I'm not the only person who owns them.*

Dave parted from the window and paced around the room. Reaching the other side, he gasped for air.

With a grimace, he returned to the window and opened it, inhaling deeply.

The suffocating sensation remained with him for a few long moments. "Now, try to calm down. Nothing has happened yet. Besides, if they considered you guilty, based on what occurred yesterday, you would already be in jail," he reasoned in the almost impossible attempt to quell his overexcited nerves. "In truth, they'd have been at your apartment this morning as they did the first time, so why don't you take a couple of deep breaths more, cool down and continue to work? You still have a lot to do, and you risk being late."

Despite the chilly weather, he decided not to close the window, not at least until he stopped experiencing that suffocating sensation.

He went to sit down at his desk, trying once again to focus on what he was doing. Luckily, he was able to complete the work in time, and as usual, at about four in the afternoon, he left the office, ready to reach the Police Department.

"Actually, it's good that I need to meet Detective Orwell," he pondered, walking to the underground station. "This way I can ask what they meant with this assertion they gave to the newspaper. I think I have the right to know what they want from me and whether they still suspect my involvement. They can't release a statement like that expecting people involved will continue to live their lives as if nothing ever happened. They don't have any right to destroy the lives of innocent people this way, so either they keep their opinions to themselves, or they tell us what they're up to."

Betrayal darkened his mood. He'd always trusted the law and the police, but now, finding himself threatened, his trust started to vacillate, and resentment got a foothold in his heart.

Immersed in his considerations and without even realizing it, he reached the Police Department and hesitated for a moment to think, trying to get a hold of his emotions.

He closed his eyes, took a couple of deep breaths, and as soon as his heartbeat returned to the regular pace, he resumed his pacing toward the building's entrance.

Despite what he feared, nobody was waiting for him. Everybody seemed to mind their own business.

He walked to the reception desk and asked to be announced to Detective Orwell, who, hopefully, was the only one expecting him.

As the receptionist hung up the phone, she smiled at Dave. "He will be here soon."

"Thanks," Dave muttered in reply, glancing around. In his visual tour, he appreciated the details of the interior as a way to pass the time before the arrival of Detective Orwell.

"Sorry to make you wait. Time went by fast today, as I was busy." A voice interrupted his random thoughts and Kane appeared from behind, apologizing.

"No problem. I understand." A wary smile brightened Dave's face.

He was still waiting for the trap they'd prepared to arrest him for snapping around him. "So, please come with me to my office, where we can talk more comfortably." Dave hesitated, pulling a couple of steps backward.

He wanted to give him the drawing and leave, as an uncomfortable knot formed in his stomach.

Recalling all the remnants of his self-control, he fought that sensation and pushed it back, displaying an apparent calm covering his inner turmoil.

As they reached the office, Kane allowed Dave to come in and closed the door behind him. "I suppose you brought me the drawing with the message Ms. Burroughs left on your mailbox," Kane guessed, glancing at the sheet Dave was holding in his hand.

With a small jolt as if the sheet suddenly materialized in his hand, he raised it and smiled. "Yes, here." He placed it on the table.

"We will need to isolate all the foreign particles, and that means we need to take your fingerprints and extract your DNA so everything else will be identified as Gloria's traces or whoever else's," Kane explained, putting on a pair of latex gloves and inserting the sheet of paper in a clear bag.

"Of course, I... I understand," Dave hesitated, fearing it meant also taking his DNA to connect him to the crime scene. *Thinking about it, this could be the final proof I'm foreign to the murders.*

"Is there anything wrong?" Kane asked, observing Dave's reaction.

"No, I was pondering something else. I understand it and I think it's a great idea," Dave reassured, nodding nervously.

"Perfect, then you need to follow me upstairs. There's our forensic lab, where we can take all the samples we might need." Kane stood from the chair.

They started to walk silently to the elevators, and as they were waiting, Dave grabbed all his courage and glanced at Kane. "I was reading today about the statement given by the police about those murders which happened in my neighborhood," Dave commenced.

"Huh... what about it?"

"Well according to the article, they arrested a few suspects and although some of them were released for lack of evidence, they might still be questioned about it.

The way I understand it, I might still be deemed guilty of murder..."

"Fear not," Kane jested. "The statement should be interpreted as those like you who have been freed, are considered innocent, but they might play a role in testifying against the real murderer. If this was the reason for your concern, you should stop worrying."

"I might do so, but in my office, people took it the wrong way. According to the glances I received today, my connection to the murders was confirmed, whether direct or not. This also means I might lose my job if people start to raise their concerns about their perception of safety. An editor is easily replaced," he was outraged by the ease with which they spat their statements without bothering to explain what they actually meant.

The misunderstanding could cost him dearly, but it appeared they didn't give a damn. "In such a case, I suggest you find a lawyer, because this isn't a valid reason to be fired. You're not a suspect anymore. You're now a witness, so you have nothing to do with any criminal activity, at least not this one," Kane replied as they reached the door of the laboratory.

The whole process didn't take more than a few minutes and soon enough, Dave and Kane returned to Kane's office.

"I hope we can extract some more information from the analysis of the drawing, but I must admit you're a talented artist." Kane tried to release the tension obviously transpiring from Dave's movements.

"Thanks, it's simply a hobby."

"Well, perhaps if you lose your job at the newspaper, you might find another as a cartoonist. But coming back to the drawing, you gave her three of your drawings. Now the fact that she chose and returned that particular one might give us a clue about what happened to her. Either it was a way to tell you who was behind her, or what she feared so much to make her decide to leave within one day without even telling you anything," Kane considered, taking a seat in his chair.

"I'll go through the results of the lab analysis and see what I can get out of them. I'll let you know when I find something worth sharing."

"I appreciate your help, although I wish to have more time and participate more actively in the search," Dave dared.

Kane closed his eyes and shook his head, smirking. "Believe me, the fewer involved, the better the chances to find Ms. Burroughs. I understand your feelings, but this is something you will have to leave to me."

Biting his lower lip, wishing to withdraw his last sentence, he lowered his glance to his feet. "You're right, it was a stupid thought. I'll wait for your news, then."

"I'll try to keep you updated as frequently as possible. Would this work better for you?" Kane proposed.

A grateful smile appeared on Dave's lips, as shyly he raised his gaze one more time before leaving the room. "Yes, it will help me a lot. At least it will make me less anxious."

"This is my job, and I'll do all I can to find her. Take care and don't worry too much about your situation. There aren't any accusations against you."

Dave exhaled, relieved. "Thank you very much. See you." He reached the building at about seven o'clock in the evening.

With a fast glance he toured visually the streets, which started to become populated with those same faces who ruled the blocks during the night, and sometimes also during the day, depending on the business they were after.

However, for the Christmas period, among the criminal element, there was a sort of respect for this kind of festivity and their actions were limited and less violent than during the rest of the year.

Yet, the term 'less violent' didn't indicate they weren't terrorizing the neighborhood, dealing drugs, weapons, and human beings.

It meant they did it to a lesser extent. It makes me sick; things must go this way in this part of the city.

This shouldn't happen at all, not here or anywhere else... he thought, pushing open the front door of the building where he lived. He turned his glance back to the street.

A couple of kids played the tough guys to impress those who arrived with their fancy rides at the same moment.

He knew them all; their parents worked their asses off on double shifts to keep them in school, but there was no way to keep them from being in the streets after dark.

"Don't you two need to go to school tomorrow?" Dave yelled, trying to call them back.

The boys turned their annoyed glances at him, but unexpectedly, instead of ignoring him, they walked back home, following him.

Dave wondered whether this was some sort of reaction to the possible general suspicion that he was the mysterious avenger.

Perhaps Shauna wasn't wrong when she said this is what they need to keep the kids away from the streets.

Maybe when she suggested I could at least pretend to be the avenger, she meant only that, Dave thought, closing the door behind them as they came inside the building. "You should keep yourself far from those thugs. They're not as cool as they want you to think they are, and their lives are not going to be much longer, after all," Dave warned.

"Because then you will kill them?" one of them wondered.

"Because living dangerously involves bigger risks, and those are not worth being taken. Your families are working hard to give you a chance for a better life; you should grab the opportunity while you can, because once the train has gone, you won't be given another possibility and those guys outside will never be there for anyone else but themselves. Now let's go back home, shall we?"

"My mom hasn't returned yet, and my dad works on the night shift," complained one of them.

"So does mine..." added the other. Dave sighed.

"Then let's do something. We're going to write a message to your mothers and leave it on the doors. Then we're going to my apartment and try to figure out something to eat. How about it?"

The two boys winked at each other, excited to spend the night with the guy they all called *'the avenger.'*

He wasn't into having children hanging around in his house. But maybe he thought, I could entertain them with my drawings, and if they wanted, they could keep some of them.

Kids love superheroes, and perhaps they will be inspired by those I'm drawing every day. With his big surprise, the two boys, Ron and Ben, (those were their names), behaved nicely and were indeed impressed by his artistic skills.

Their mothers returned after a couple of hours, thankful to realize they had been kept away from the streets by the avenger himself, or the one they considered so.

"I try to get home as soon as I can, but working on the other side of the city means I'm bottled up in a traffic jam almost every day. I'm grateful for what you did today; I know you weren't supposed to take care of them, and we never agreed upon this sort of babysitting..." Ben's mother tried to explain.

"Life isn't going to be easy. I personally can't wait for the time when he'll be ready to leave to go and live on his own, once Ron will go to college, but there is still a long way until then, and what scares me the most is when he will be a teenager. You know, at their age you need to rebel against all sorts of rules and regulations, and I'm afraid life on the streets will become the answer to their questions, in particular when the question is freedom," Ron's mother added, shaking her head hopelessly.

"What can I say? Perhaps you should involve them more in solving the problems at home. Let them participate in the discussions between adults, and they will never feel the need to search for freedom. Maybe all you need to do is to listen to what they have to say," Dave tried to suggest, knowing that he didn't hold any knowledge or experience whatsoever in raising children.

One thing he could say was he remembered once he was one of them, and being kept aside from the decisions in the family didn't help him to develop the self-confidence that distinguished successful people like Kane, or Alan.

"Thank you, we will try to follow your suggestions, but now we need to go," Ron's mother replied, glancing at the children. "Come on guys, we need to go back home. Tomorrow you're going to school."

The two kids huffed, not willing to go back home, but tired enough to go straight to bed. "Once again, thank you for your patience. Good night," the two mothers said.

When Dave was finally alone, he drew a long breath. Exhausted, he closed his eyes, tilting his head backward.

He thanked God there weren't any children to complicate his messed-up life. For some long moments, he remained in his position, trying to regain some inner peace.

As soon as he felt better, he turned his gaze at the drawing he'd made for the kids and a chuckle escaped his mouth. "Maybe I should talk to Detective Orwell about the possibility to pretend to be the avenger..." He shook his head. "What a stupid idea! Pretending to be someone you're not, and even on the wrong side of the law. I must've gone crazy!"

He glanced around and considered the mess that happened in his apartment. "Now, here there would be the need for a superhero of the cleanings, and I guess the only one in this room is me." With a shake of his head, he started to put things in order.

Since the last time he cleaned in depth, he'd made every effort to be sure the place kept the appearance of tidiness, where everything had its place and was easy to find.

After an hour, he walked around and made a visual tour of the apartment, trying to spot anything that wasn't in place. His bedroom was the last place he checked.

The door of the closet grabbed his attention, for it was open – the closet where he kept, besides his clothes, the suitcase with the coat he wore the previous evening to see whether he could have fit the image of his newly created superhero.

He placed it back inside and locked the door. Then, satisfied with the result, he went to sleep, hoping for a better day the morning after.

His night didn't pass as quietly as he hoped; his sleep was cursed by nightmares about his workplace, Gloria, Ben, and Ron, but most of all there was the Humphrey Bogart man and his evil counterpart, that dark figure everybody swore having seen at every crime scene.

***

He woke up a few minutes before the alarm clock and felt grateful to realize it was a dream, yet it was able to leave him with bitterness in his mouth.

"I need to find Gloria. I believe she's the key to my sanity and if I can't find her, or at least be sure she's safe and sound, I'll go crazy," he stood from his bed.

He went to open the blinds of the window and check the weather for the day.

"Fog," he mumbled acknowledging the white curtain blanketing the whole city. "The perfect climate for a superhero, for my Man from the Mist, or perhaps I should call him Misty Man." He chuckled on his way to get a shower.

He was in an excellent mood and ready to face another working day, wondering what would happen.

I hope the news of yesterday had been clarified, I'm not a suspect for the murder, and if they still doubt, I think I will ask Detective Orwell to intervene and explain the situation before it becomes unbearable, Dave thought.

He tried to sneak to his office unnoticed like he always did in the past. The difference was that, although in the past nobody would have detected him, this time he felt like he was continually in the spotlight.

However, instead of being admired the way Joseph was, he received cold glances, gazes blaming him for being a killer.

Perhaps they also feared he would kill them too. I admit nobody would like to work together with a person who is suspected to be a serial killer, but if this man has been unfairly charged with something he never did, then people should take his part.

They should get close to him and sympathize with his situation. Instead, here I find nothing but hostility, blame, and fear.

I wish I lived somewhere else, or perhaps to be someone else," he thought striding to the hall to reach his office.

CHAPTER 9

"Stanford..." The voice of the director of the newspaper resounded in the corridor, echoing like a rumble of distant thunder.

Dave turned himself in the direction of the voice, locking his glance on him. "Good morning, Mr. Anders."

"Good morning," Mr. Anders greeted, "Can you come to my office for a moment? I need to talk to you before you start your work."

"Of course." He followed Mr. Anders, fully aware that bad news waited for him there, as it never happened before that he'd been called by the director for pleasantries.

As soon as they entered the room, Mr. Anders closed the door and invited him to sit down.

"Mr. Stanford, I do believe you're already aware of the reason why I asked you here." His hands entwined before him as if to create a barrier between them.

"To be honest, no." The way he bit his lower lip betrayed his confusion, as he sat down on the chair in front of the desk. Mr. Anders groaned, wondering where to start.

"How are you dealing with the accusations raised by the police?" At his question, it became clear the thunder he heard from afar just reached him, hovering his head, and soon enough, he realized it was about to storm.

Despite that, he recalled the assurance of Kane about the possibility of losing his job. "Yesterday I met with Detective Orwell, and I questioned him about my situation. He assured me that, although I was taken to the Department for interrogation, they didn't find any evidence that binds me to any of the crime scenes."

He paused, hearing the flickering in his voice. "Therefore, like a few others who had been arrested, I was released, and I'm not considered a suspect anymore, but a witness. Jonathan failed to mention this detail in the text I edited, and I'm afraid it's going to give the wrong impression of me," Dave tried to explain.

He feared because of the article, people started to demand his resignation from the job.

"I understand, and you're right about the chaos a misunderstanding creates in this sort of situation. Nevertheless, I can't disregard the tension among the working staff, and as a director I need to take care of the well-being of every employee. You're a skilled and hard-working editor; it would be a mistake to fire you on the grounds of those latest happenings, but I have to consider not only your needs, but those of everyone else too." Mr. Anders took a short pause to be sure Dave understood what he meant.

Indeed, Dave realized the meaning of his words, yet he still considered the treatment he was receiving unfair, and he wanted to make sure the director was fully aware of the weight of his words on Dave's life.

"What do you mean?" He cocked his head to the side

"I checked your working schedule. You didn't take all the holidays you were entitled to, not to mention the extra hours. This means you accumulated about a couple of months, which I hope you will be willing to take now. Most likely, after this period, the situation will be solved and forgotten. When you come back, you will start from where you left and continue your life as usual," Mr. Anders proposed.

I bet he asked around about the possibility of firing me, but as this would have not been legal, he decided to keep me far from the others. Indeed, this gives me the chance to search for Gloria on my own. Perhaps if the police are looking in one direction, and I'm looking in the other, we might be able to find her.

Dave glared at Mr. Anders. He wasn't satisfied with the solution proposed, but maybe there wasn't any other choice to make everybody happy. "I will take time off. Can I at least finish this day?"

"I would prefer if you'd leave right away, but since you're already here, you can carry on the most important tasks and go at noon. What do you think?" Mr. Anders proposed, trying to reach a compromise between the urgent requests of the other employees, and Dave's right to be treated fairly.

A frown creased his forehead. He realized Dave's struggle in the workplace; not being a popular person on the team resulted in becoming the scapegoat for every problem.

I believe if this had happened to another guy, to one of the most admired ones, all the rest of the team would have gathered together to support him emotionally. In Dave's case, nobody cares about him, and he will be chosen as a sacrificial lamb to please the gods. How sad, Mr. Anders pondered, observing his expression.

"Of course, Mr. Anders. I will now go to my office and leave at noon. I'll be in touch with you in a couple of months, and we shall analyze the developments of the situation," Dave tried to swallow his bitterness and anger.

"Thanks for your understanding. I wish you a pleasant resting period. This can be a good chance to catch up with your private life, friends, and family. I'm sure your girlfriend will be pleased." A cheerful smile appeared on his face in an attempt to force Dave to look at the bright side.

"I bet she will." Growling, he stood up, ready to leave the office.

He walked the hall under the surveillance of the curious gazes of his colleagues.

They followed him with their eyes, quite surprised when they realized he headed to his office instead of leaving the building. Alan, too, glanced at him, and different from the others, he smiled.

Like all the rest of the world, he'd never acknowledged his presence. For him, Dave was only a name on the list of the group emails sent.

The latest events which brought Dave under the spotlight made him reconsider what he thought. When Dave faced Joseph like he had nothing to lose, Alan realized that over the years, he failed to befriend an enticing person.

He sensed, behind his façade of gray existence, a spark needed to come to light. Dave, in his office, instead started to cry.

He'd reached the bottom of his own life; being kept far from his job was the worst news he could have ever expected.

Although he hadn't been fired, they treated him like a disease. All he wanted was to be left in peace to live his life; even if solitary, gray, and insignificant, he missed how it used to be.

I never wanted to be a superhero, but I never wanted to become a villain either. I haven't killed anyone, nor am I planning to. Yet, people around me can't wait to seize the chance to jump over me like hungry beasts. "Why me?" he sobbed aloud.

He grabbed his head between his hands and tried to stop crying, but the bitterness and the stress he gathered overwhelmed him, and perhaps he wouldn't be able to edit anything for the day.

A river of tears accumulated during all the years of his life needed to flood away, and he decided not to hold the flow any longer.

It took a bit more than an hour worth of sobbing, but tired or finally relieved, his thoughts were more defined, and a shy smile arched the corners of his mouth upward.

"I guess I accumulated too much negativity without ever discharging it anywhere, and now it needed to be released," he dried his eyes. "I think I'll need to wait some time before thinking about going to get coffee. I must resemble one of my villains with these red eyes."

A weak chuckle escaped him, so he decided to start to work on something small, to bring it to completion before the time he left the office. "I might also skip the coffee for today. When all the others are at lunch break, my deserved vacation will begin."

A few minutes passed by, and his attention was focused on the text to edit, when someone knocked unexpectedly at his door.

"Y-Yes?" he answered, surprised.

Alan's face gingerly peeked through the crack of the door left ajar. "Do you mind if I come in for a chat?"

"I... No, I don't... Why?" Dave tried to figure out whether he was having a hallucination or there was indeed Alan asking to come in for a chat.

With a self-confident smile, he entered the room and closed the door behind him. "I thought you were having a rough time, and maybe it's also my fault. Did he fire you?"

"No, I got the chance to take all the holidays and the extra time I skipped. I'll be away for about two months starting from today at noon," Dave replied, relaxing.

"That's a relief, and perhaps it would be good for everybody, but most of all for you. I believe you need some time to understand what you want and how to reach it. I'm guilty like all the others for not having tried to get to know you. Until now, we had no idea you were working here, and we'd continued to ignore your presence until something happened." Alan grabbed a chair from one side of the wall and brought it close to his desk.

"I don't need any charity, nor any fake friendship. If you're in trouble with your conscience, you should talk to a priest, not to me. At the end of this day, I'll go out of this office and be away for the next two months. I'm not sure whether I will return. Perhaps I'll be fired. This is because you all prefer to judge me as guilty." He could taste the bitterness in his words and took a short pause as if to swallow a foul medicine.

"But this is not a question of being safe, it's an excuse to get rid of a rather annoying presence. A popular guy like Joseph, although he's an asshole, will always be excused for every shitty behavior he will take," he clasped his hands together. "A person like me, an anonymous gray bog, is something nobody wants to have close by. I don't understand them, but this is how the world goes. I don't care what they say about me. I don't need to. My life is miserable the way it is, and now you can leave me alone and go tell all the others what kind of loser I am. Have a fat laugh at my expense but save me your pathetic excuses." The tone of his voice remained calm, but the fury inside was palpable.

Alan goggled at him, open-mouthed. "Wow, I was right."

"Right about what?" Dave sneered.

"You're indeed a brilliant person. I admit having failed in going beyond appearances, but you should show your colors to the world, because as I see now, you're a superstar." Alan stood from the chair, ready to leave.

At the door, he turned to glance at Dave. "By the way, if you like bowling, you can find me at the Paradise Bowl close to the railway station. I go there every Friday. It's quite a stress reliever. I might enjoy some company from time to time, so if you want to join me, I'll be there the day after tomorrow at five o'clock in the evening. Otherwise, I will play a couple of rounds against myself."

Without waiting for any reply from Dave, he was ready to leave. "Alan..." he called.

"Yes?"

"Thanks." A broad smile appeared on his face. "I'll see you soon." Alan winked, closing the door behind him.

"Perhaps I need a friend," Dave whispered. After all, maybe that day was not going so wrong.

He wondered whether he could trust Alan; unable to find any reason not to, he considered joining him at bowling.

Glancing at the clock, there were still a couple of hours before the end of his day and he decided to use them to finish what he started.

***

In his office, Kane tried to find anything to connect the clues with one another, but besides the connection between Gloria and the Fedora man, there wasn't anything that helped to solve that mystery.

I'm missing something I can't grasp. Obviously, she wanted to escape him because he threatened her, but the unsolved question is why didn't she ask Dave for help? I do believe he would have done everything in his power to protect her, unless she was sure she'd have brought him into the same danger she was into.

He stood up and started to walk in circles around the room. "What if she was also afraid of Dave? What if the fedora man doesn't exist, but it was Dave who stalked her?" Kane wondered.

"No! That man was already after her when she was living in another city. The most possible reason is she wanted to avoid dragging Dave into her same misery. Perhaps she was forced to follow this guy under the threat of harming Dave. That's why she left a sort of clue in Dave's mailbox. A sketch representing the silhouette of a man on a misty day."

He stopped walking for a second, recalling the drawing. "A man... on... a foggy day? Maybe this is a lead. This freak who stalked her appeared only with the haze?"

He hesitated in the middle of the room, with his hand caressing the stubble on his chin. "Some hint! Here the fog rises almost every day in winter. I need to check the climate records, either for the times when the murders of the drug dealers happened and for the time when she disappeared. If I'm lucky, we can gather another clue and a freak."

Kane rushed back to sit down at his desk, switching on his laptop, browsing the weather station's recording for those days. "I think I'll need to ask Dave some other questions. He might know what kind of weather it was when he realized Gloria was missing, because if I recall it right, he mentioned something about a man coming out of the building the same day of her departure. I don't know whether he was searching for any clue she left behind, or it was a way to acknowledge that she moved away..."

He started to browse the weather records. "Hmm... the whole period has been foggy, so this can mean everything and nothing. Again, I'm back at the start."

His thoughts were interrupted by the telephone ringing. "Orwell," he replied.

"Good evening, Detective," greeted Jenna Lee from the forensics lab. "Are you still in your office?"

"Yes, but I was thinking about going home. It's starting to get late and I'm beginning to get quite frustrated."

"Then great news is waiting for you," she chirped happily. "And if you come upstairs, I can also give you the results and the report about what we've found."

Kane jumped from his chair. He had been sure it would take longer to reach any conclusive results on the drawing, and Jenna gave him a spark of hope which brightened his evening. "I'll be there in a sec," he hanged up the conversation.

She remained for a moment to stare at her telephone. "This is what I call being excited by the news."

After less than a minute, Kane slammed open the door of the lab, panting like he'd been running a marathon. "What's the news?" he breathed.

"Take it easy, I'm not going anywhere," she giggled, grabbing a chair. "Here, sit down and regain your breath or you'll pass out."

"I know, but I'm quite desperate. The more information I add to this case, the more complicated it turns out," Kane whispered, inhaling a few times deeply.

"Well, the interesting thing is that besides, of course, the DNA of Mr. Stanford, which was expected, as he was the one who did the drawing, we could identify another two different traces. One, a trace of sweat, belongs to a woman, and the other isn't identified, meaning we don't have enough material, but most certainly three people have been in touch with the paper," she started to explain. "The woman is probably the missing girl, as she was the one who received it. We were also able to isolate her fingerprints. The other could be a man or a woman, as we could separate only an incomplete sample of fingerprints. It won't be easy, but if this person is in our archives, we might start looking for him or her."

Kane smiled as his heartbeat reached a reasonable pace. "That's indeed amazing. At least we have a starting point. I hope we'll find that individual. Although it's not certain we'll find him or her, this is a detail to be added to the puzzle."

"There's more." Jenna raised a finger in mid-air. "We also examined the handwriting of the girl and compared it with the one on the form she filled out when taking possession of the keys of the apartment. The text *'I'm sorry'* was written in a hurry and in a tense emotional state. Possibly, she was afraid of something or someone who could reach and harm her. Now, the point where I would focus my attention is whether she could run away.... this time."

"That man followed her wherever she moved."

"Did you check the moving companies or car rentals? If she had to move her stuff, even if leaving by leaps and bounds, she needed to use one of those services," Jenna wondered.

"I already checked." Kane shook his head. "She didn't book any such service, nor had there been any car rental in her name. At this moment, there are two chances: the first is that a friend lent her a van or rented one in his name, in order not to leave a trace. In this case, we think she was able to escape, finding a new place to stay. The second option is she had been threatened and forced to follow the stalker who cleared the apartment not to raise any suspicion."

After a short pause, he resumed his considerations. "As by routine, we circulated the information of a missing girl, but so far nobody has seen her, so I might be prone to believe she decided to move away and wrote the last message to Dave using one of the drawings he gave her as a present. She returned the keys to the superintendent of the building, and when she hoped she could make it and run away, the mysterious guy appeared and kidnapped her," his voice turned into a muttering sound.

"She was brought away. The kidnapper took care of clearing the place of her stuff to make it appear as if she moved away. He provided the spotless cleaning of the apartment to clear any possible evidence, and now we have a woman who has disappeared into the night." Kane took a deep breath, trying to put some order to his thoughts.

Jenna nodded. "Then we just need to compare those fingerprints we've found with those in our records and in the National Database and hope you'll find a match. I'll send you the data immediately so you can start right away to find a matching person and give a name to the possible kidnapper/stalker. Although, it might also be that those fingerprints belong to someone else who isn't involved in the missing of this girl."

"I hope to find something, but most of all I wish to find the girl." Kane stood up from the chair, ready to leave. "I'll be waiting downstairs for the data you've collected and the report. If I need more information..."

"You will ask me tomorrow morning, as now I'm going home. I also suggest you follow my example, or you will soon burnout, and you won't be of any help to anybody, especially to yourself," Jenna interrupted him.

"How can I relax and go home when there is an intricate mystery to solve? Particularly when, like in this case, there is the life of a person at stake." Kane paced away.

She watched him leaving and shook her head. "As you wish, but don't come to tell me I haven't warned you," she whispered, as she went to the computer to send all the documentation to his email before going home.

Walking toward his office, he ruminated about the results of the lab tests.

Possibly, the solution to the riddle might lie in the choice of the drawing. I believe that although she was in a hurry, she should have had at hand other pieces of paper. The fact that she chose one of the sketches should mean something; likewise the choice between the three drawings should have a meaning. What I'm wondering is what were the others representing?

***

Dave was trying to distract his thoughts from the day he had by watching a bit of TV.

He wasn't following anything that was coming from there, but he liked to have it on so he wouldn't feel the weight of his loneliness.

The calm of his house was abruptly interrupted by the ringing of his telephone, and an unknown number appeared on the screen.

"Hello..." Dave lazily replied.

"Good evening, Mr. Stanford, this is Detective Orwell. I hope I'm not calling at an inopportune time."

"Good evening, Officer, you don't disturb me at all. I was watching TV, but to be honest, I wasn't following anything that happened. Do you have any news to share with me about Gloria?" Dave switched off the TV.

"Yes and no. I got the results from the lab, and it seems like, besides your fingerprints and DNA, which was expected, they could find two other sets of traces. One belongs to Gloria, most likely. The others cannot yet be identified.

"Since the test on the organic material was inconclusive, we don't know if the person in question was a female or a male. Nevertheless, we isolated the fingerprints, and I'm going to search in the archive whether I can find a match to identify and isolate the girl's traces," Kane explained, drumming his fingers on the table. "However, the real reason why I called you is to ask you what kind of drawings you gave to Gloria. You told me that she chose three of them. One represented that figure walking on a foggy day, but what were the other two representing?"

Dave remained for a moment silent, trying to bring them back to his memory. "I'm not sure. I draw so many characters and it's not easy to recall everything, but let me think about it for a moment."

Standing from the couch, he went to grab his sketchbook. He hoped that by browsing the drawings he had, he could remember what she took.

Kane waited patiently without saying a word, holding his breath in anticipation.

Those details might seem irrelevant, and he feared that Dave forgot about them. "I think one of them was a sketch of the small lake in the park. She liked the drawing because it was peaceful and reminded her about a lazy Sunday afternoon. The other one, it was a portrait of a woman I think I saw in my dreams; mostly I draw about what comes to my mind, whether superheroes, dreams that impressed me, or more rarely places I visit. That park is a place I go for a jog," Dave explained, flipping the pages of the sketchbook.

"Do you remember if you might have been inspired by this Humphrey Bogart guy to have sketched that figure?" Kane pursued, leaning on the chair and glancing at the ceiling.

"It's possible..." Dave tried to recall whether that drawing was done before or after Gloria arrived. *Of course, this would explain a lot.*

He glanced at the previous drawings, forcing his memory to go back to the time he drew, or if he could find something that could have given him a hint about the date.

I need to focus on if I drew this before the appearance of that mysterious man. If so, then either I'm a clairvoyant, I'm the avenger just like everybody believes, or this is a strange coincidence. A figure walking on a foggy day is a vivid and evocative image, and all the heroes have at least once walked away, disappearing in the mist, but was this the case? Dave wondered.

"I can't say now. I need to think about it and go through all the drawings, trying to recall a detail that can put a couple of them on a specific date and determine whether they had been drawn before or after the arrival of Gloria or of this mysterious man," Dave replied, shaking his head, as nothing seemed to come clear in his mind.

"I understand," Kane's lips pressed tight into a grimace.

He hoped to obtain an answer to his question, but he also knew people rarely put a date on everything they do, because one day they might become useful when a friend gets kidnapped or is missing.

"I'm sorry not to be able to help you right now, but I promise I'll go through each drawing in this sketchbook, and I hope I can find a way to date at least one of them," Dave apologized. "Wait a minute! Couldn't the lab find the answer to this question? Haven't they searched for this?"

Kane felt almost like an idiot for not having thought about this detail. "If you ever need another job, let me know. This is a brilliant observation! I didn't read their report in full, but I haven't requested an analysis of the ink, either. I was so focused on getting information about those who handled that sheet of paper that I forgot the evidence. I'll go through the whole report and eventually, I'll send them back the drawing and ask for a dating based on the ink."

He could see the light at the end of the tunnel. Of course, this doesn't solve the case, but it might help them view things from a different perspective.

If Gloria chose to write the message on that sketch, which represented the eventual kidnapper/stalker or whatever else, then they had the first clue to the identity of the man they had to search for.

It seemed like that drawing was more than the first sheet of paper she found to leave him a quick note.

At that point, it was an invaluable clue that could give a solution not only to the missing of Gloria, but maybe also to the murders of those drug dealers.

Dave squeezed in his shoulders. "Well, perhaps I'll need a new job within a couple of months."

"Why? Did they fire you?"

"Not quite, but the pressures put on the director by the rest of the staff was enough to make him come to the decision to remove me for at least a period of time. He asked me to take all my vacation I forgot to take, together with the extra hours that I accumulated," Dave explained.

"But this doesn't mean that you'll be fired. As I told you, this isn't a valid reason to fire someone, particularly because you're not a suspect anymore. Under the right circumstances, this is something that can happen to anyone. It's sufficient to be at the right place at the wrong time. When a murder is committed in an apartment, unless there is clear evidence of the crime, every tenant of the building is a potential suspect. This is bullshit," Kane growled, surprised by Dave's revelation.

"I know, but I'm not a popular person on the team. As I told you, I have been invisible for most of my life, and particularly at work. I wonder whether anyone recalls my name. To tell the truth, one guy, Alan, came to me apologizing for not having tried to get to know me better. He admitted that nobody acknowledged my presence before, but as soon as I became suspected of multiple murder, my invisibility offered them a confirmation of guilt. I hope my employer is right when he says that within a couple of months everybody will hardly recall the reason why I was away, and my life will continue the way it used to be." Kane nodded.

"I guess he's right, and probably also for you, this absence from work can be beneficial. Perhaps you'll find out that you need to move on."

"I'm a guy who doesn't like surprises and changes. I would prefer to return to my gray, anonymous existence, although in that case, I would love to receive news about Gloria."

"We'll do everything we can to find her..."

Dave tried to smile. "I know you will, and I trust you..."

That evening, sleep didn't want to come to release the tension of the day. If he were living in a calmer area, he would consider going out for a jog.

Perhaps he could reach the park, even if it was dark, but when the sun went down, going outside was an action that required the acknowledgment of the risks involved.

From the streets, the first noises caused by the coming and going of the cars of drug dealers, together with the casual fights between them and those who came to buy either for themselves or for their own business, started to fill the calm of the night.

He wondered whether either the criminals or the people living there still believed in an avenger who would clean the whole neighborhood of those thugs. Indeed, something must change.

The city can't believe that by restricting the criminals to a specific area equals defeating them and having successfully provided for the citizens' safety, Dave thought.

"We're citizens too. We also go to work and pay our taxes, and we all deserve to have our rights defended, even if we're not wealthy," he said aloud.

He peeked out from the window. Now the fog was thick, and it was almost impossible to see who you were walking against.

He glanced at the scattered beams coming from the streetlamps and the traffic lights. It was almost surreal, and he thought about that man in the mist. "This would be the time for him to appear. Soon the honest ones will be sleeping, to wake up early the morning after to go to work or to school, and in the meantime, the avenger will come to make justice of those who got terrorized, killed, raped, abducted and sold," Dave whispered, as if he could see the scene in front of his eyes.

He smiled, inspired to draw another story about his superhero. He closed the blinds and grabbed his sketchbook.

CHAPTER 10

Not being awakened up by the alarm clock on a Friday morning to go to work gave Dave a surreal sensation.

Glancing around as he stood up, he grasped another detail to add to that bizarre situation. Apparently, he fell asleep on the couch while drawing his character, and sleepwalking, he managed to drop some items from the table.

Trying to focus on anything about what happened the previous night, he stood on his feet and looked around the whole place.

He couldn't remember anything apart from confused images that popped up in his mind.

One of these had something to do with the old coat he kept in his wardrobe. Walking to the bedroom to grab new clothes, his attention was caught by the door of the closet wide open and the old coat lying on the bed along with the hat.

"Did I put them on one more time?" he wondered, forcing his mind to remember.

Like coming from the fog of a drunken night, he recalled himself wearing them both. "I should stop this sort of masquerade, or one day I might also believe I'm one of my characters. This is the time I need to divide reality from the fiction of my dreams," he reproached himself, folding the coat and placing it gently in the suitcase.

"Funny thing is, I don't even recall how I came into its possession. The only thing I remember is it belonged to my grandfather. He loved it very much and used it only on special occasions," Dave considered, caressing the soft fabric. "This wool is of high quality. I don't want to think about the price of this coat, to say nothing about the fedora. Already now they're quite expensive. Think about a common guy like my grandfather. I should take care of them both, and perhaps I might also wear them whenever I have the chance... Yeah! Right, first you need a social life, something completely alien to me."

Dave stood from the bed and placed the suitcase back in the closet, still trying to figure out what happened the previous night.

After spending some time to reorder the house, he left to jog in the park. Having time on my side, I might think of coming to run every day.

Besides, this vacation can come in handy, and I wonder why I decided to let my vacation days accumulate this much, instead of using them.

Returning home, he stopped at a newsstand, attracted by the headlines of the newspaper. *For the next couple of months, this will be my only source of information. I think I should start buying papers and follow the news on TV if I want to know what's going on in this city, as well as in the rest of the world,* he pondered.

One headline, in particular, caught his attention, about the neighborhood where he lived. The mysterious avenger struck again and hit the drug dealing business to their core.

He grabbed the newspaper and started to read... "You need to buy that," growled the seller.

"Oh, yes sure," Dave shook his head and searching his pockets for the money to pay for the paper.

He walked to the bench close by and sat down reading the article. Those guys who got the attention of Ron and Ben had their lives shortened dramatically.

I hope this will make those kids understand what I meant when I said this is a life nobody should seek.

Why would someone give up his freedom, life, and integrity to follow someone else's greed and thirst for power? He thought, reading the article.

Despite the lack of any clues and no witnesses whatsoever, the shade of the avenger returned to fill the imaginations of the ordinary people.

Dave stood from the bench. "How can they draw their own conclusions about something they ignore? And what kind of journalist takes into consideration the speculation of a random bystander who is hardly aware of the fact? If they want a clear idea about what happened, they should indeed inquire about one of the members of the gang or the avenger himself."

He chuckled at the thought and wondered whether his colleague at the newspaper regretted having asked the director to kick him out. "I bet they would start to ask me about what happened since they all think I'm the killer. They lost a great opportunity for a scoop: 'Interview with the Avenger!'"

A broad smile brightened his face and, whistling, he resumed his walk. Nothing seemed to darken his mood, not even the possibility of being arrested and interrogated by the police one more time.

"Something I might want to do is to bring the coat and fedora somewhere else. In light of all the investigations, this can give me more trouble than anything else. I'm not sure whether I've ever met anyone who could afford or desire such a garment. But then again, last time they arrested me, a few officers remained to search my apartment. They must have found the suitcase, and most likely they also saw the coat and fedora. If they didn't consider it a piece of evidence, then I should be confident that those garments won't bring me any problems in the future."

When he returned home, he browsed on the internet, searching for further news about the murder and wondered about asking around whether he might find any witnesses to inquire. "They should start to understand I'm not the one who killed those criminals," he considered aloud, browsing on the web.

The ringing of the telephone caused him a sudden jolt, which sent the mouse to land on the floor on the other side of the room.

"Stanford," he answered, checking if the mouse got damaged in the impact.

"Good morning, Dave. This is Linda from the newspaper. Do you remember me?" she asked with a crystalline voice.

"If I'm not mistaken, you were one of those who asked to have me fired. Weren't you? In this case, yes, unfortunately, I do." A bitter grimace twisted the regular features of his face, knowing the reason for her call.

"Then you mistake me with someone else, but I don't mind. I understand your bitterness, and perhaps I would also be grumpy if I were you."

"So why are you calling me? Let me guess, you want to know how did I kill them? Sorry to disappoint you, but I'm innocent. Last night I spent my time drawing and watching TV until I fell asleep. This is the last thing I remember of what happened last night." "Will you ever stop that attitude?" Linda complained, annoyed.

"What are you talking about?"

"Your paranoid behavior by which everyone is plotting against you, that's what," she clarified with a miffed huff.

"That's the frame of mind the rest of the world forced me into. I've been invisible my whole life, and now I'm brought into the epicenter of a murder. The worst is that even without evidence, I passed from being the most insignificant creature on Earth to the most dangerous criminal in the world. I wish to understand how this all happened because I'm still baffled. When Joseph attacked me in the kitchen, where you, too, were present, Alan was the only one to take my side. You all were giggling at the way that fat-headed jerk humiliated me. Now I'm the one who is overreacting?"

Rage overtook his mind, and he couldn't fathom why he took out all his bitterness against Linda.

She remained silent for a moment, understanding that probably he was right, and she laughed at him for the way Joseph treated him.

Like all the others, she considered it a joke, something he should also take in the same way. He didn't...

"That was only a joke..." Her voice became almost a wheeze, hardly perceptible.

"I didn't find it funny. I wasn't laughing when he called me an 'insignificant piece of shit,'" Dave hissed, hurt.

"I shouldn't call you..." Linda cringed, regretting having even dialed his number.

"Indeed, but perhaps now we will all have the time to go over everything, and eventually one day I'll be back, and things can improve."

"I hope so, although, if you wish to leave a statement about what happened last night, you can still call me," she hoped to get at least something from calling him.

"I'll think about it." With those words, Dave ended the conversation.

He wasn't interested in hearing her voice again. If there was a newspaper which wouldn't obtain his statement, that would be the one he was working for.

They don't deserve anything, and besides, I know nothing about what happened last night. Actually, I aim to ask around if anyone has seen something, and I mean seeing, not dreaming or speculating about it, Dave thought.

Glancing around, a rumble like the peal of thunder reached his ears, reminding him of his empty stomach. With a grimace, he decided to eat something.

***

At the Police Department, things started to become hectic, and the news of a new murder didn't relieve anyone, although this meant a couple of fewer drug dealers and criminals around.

At least we're not talking about the brutal killing of an innocent person. We can't say those guys didn't look for trouble. Had they searched for an honest job, they would still be alive. Nevertheless, I don't condone anyone who seeks justice on his own, Kane thought as he paced to the lab to ask for the ink to be analyzed.

"Detective Orwell, what a surprise to have you in our humble laboratory," Jenna smirked sarcastically. "I see you brought us the sketch again. May I help you somehow?"

"You might start by cutting off your sarcasm; this isn't the right day for it," Kane growled. "Nevertheless, yesterday you said the real clue might be on the drawing itself, rather than on the DNA traces or on the message. I have been thinking about it for the whole evening, and I wondered whether it was made before the mysterious stalker arrived or after."

"Killjoy!" she exclaimed, throwing her hands in the air. "Did you try asking the artist?"

"Yes, and he doesn't recall, so I thought to bring it back to you. Can we analyze the ink and extrapolate a sort of dating for the drawing?" He wasn't sure if this was something they could carry out in their laboratory, or whether it was something possible at all.

Yet, it seemed to be such a good idea that it was worth at least trying.

"Hmm..." Jenna narrowed her eyes, humming. "We cannot tell the exact date, but if you tell me an age frame we might try."

"Let me think about it. I believe we need to know whether he drew it before October or after."

"Can we have the pen he used for this sketch?" She thought about also having the original ink being tested for better calibration.

Kane grabbed his mobile phone from the pocket of his jeans. "I will tell you in a moment."

Dave had just finished eating his lunch when once again the telephone started to ring. "I've never been so popular in my whole entire life. Two calls in a day! I'm up for a personal record."

"Stanford," he answered.

"Good afternoon, this is Detective Orwell, and I'm now at the lab, asking for ink dating on your drawing. Do you still have the same pen you drew this one with?" Kane asked, immediately skipping all the pleasantries.

"Yes, I always use the same one and the same brand ink. I wish I had money to buy more and a different kind of them, but so far, so bad. Do you want me to bring it to you at the Police Department?"

"I would be extremely grateful." Kane winked victoriously at Linda.

"Fine, if you can give me about an hour, I'll bring you all you need. Will I meet you in the hall?" He glanced at the clock on his laptop and considered the time it would take for him to reach them.

"Yes, I'll be waiting for you, but if you think you're running late, give me a call."

"Of course, see you soon, then. Bye." Kane ended the conversation and turned his gaze at Linda. "He will be here with the pen he uses within an hour. How much time does this kind of process take?"

"Let me think. Analyzing the original, sampling the old one... between two days and one week; I hope you're not expecting it sooner," she counted on her fingers.

"I can wait. The only thing I'm wondering is whether you need only a specimen of the ink he used, or you need the whole pen."

"Just a sample would be enough, I guess."

"Perfect, so in the meantime, you can have the drawing." He handed her the paper inside a clear, sealed folder. "As soon as possible I will return with all the material Dave will bring me."

Returning to his office, the blinking on the screen informed him of a message coming from the call center in his email, and apparently someone called, answering the ad for a missing person they'd sent out all over the country.

He called reception to retrieve the name, surname, and telephone number of the caller. *If I can at least give him some great news about Gloria... Recently he only received terrible news: First, his friend disappears; second, he's accused of murder; then he lost his job. I need to cheer him up.*

Dave had the time to finish his lunch and grabbed his pen, leaving to reach the Police Department.

Quite soon, it would be Christmas, and he wondered whether the investigation to find Gloria would also experience an interruption to be resumed after the holidays.

I guess Detective Orwell would take some time off for a holiday, but likewise, everybody at the Police Department would be on call whenever his presence is required, Dave thought, at the main door of the building.

The weather didn't improve, and the same gloomy sky was upon the world. Although, in his neighborhood, everything appeared darker than in any other part of the city.

Probably because of the degraded infrastructure for which the municipality didn't consider worth refurbishing when upgrading other areas that involved the possibility of a potential economic return.

He was immersed in his considerations when unexpectedly, from a secondary road, someone grabbed him and slammed him against the wall.

"We've started losing patience. The 'Boss' didn't appreciate you playing the superhero." The man talking to him was at least double Dave's size, but what petrified him the most was the touch with the blade of a knife right at his neck.

His heart began to pound as if it wanted to break free from the cage of his chest. Breathless, he couldn't utter a single word and closed his eyes, waiting for the maniac to bring his act to completion and kill him.

"I... I don't know what you're talking about..." he finally whispered, gathering the last bits of air left in his lungs.

"Fuck you do!" he yelled pressing the blade closer. "Now stop interfering with our business or your body will be found scattered all around the road between your house and the Police Department, and I'm not sure whether you will be dead when we dump you there. Did I make myself clear?"

"You got the wrong man," Dave whispered, fearing they believed the rumor according to which he was the mysterious avenger. "I'm not responsible for the murder of your people... I... I can't..."

"I don't care. You make sure this is going to stop here!" That said, the man left and flashed himself back to the secondary road from where he came.

Dave's knees became weak and unable to sustain him. He fell on the hard concrete floor, gasping for air and paralyzed by fear.

His body was frozen on the ground, confident of being close to death. He was not the avenger and had no power to block something someone else had started.

After an interminable amount of time, he could stand on his feet, and he wondered whether he would be able to reach the Police Department in time or alive.

In despair he didn't know what he was supposed to do. *How can I stop something I didn't start?* Suddenly, he recalled the way he woke up in the morning.

The coat was not in the same place where he'd placed it the day before; it was lying on his bed. The craziest idea swirled in his mind and panic rose from the innermost part of his soul.

He heard before of cases of split personality, and the doubt of him really being the avenger just as a sort of Dr. Jekyll froze the blood in his veins. He glanced frantically around himself, as if someone was hiding behind him and listening to his thoughts, so he could run to the police.

What am I supposed to do? If I say anything about what happened I will be arrested for murder. It will be like a confession. Besides, I can't risk getting killed by those gangs, and if I don't receive any help, maybe one day I might be dangerous to innocent people too...

Pinching his lips together, he needed to find some time to reach a solution on his own without asking anyone to intervene. *I'll try to find out first whether I'm the one who killed those criminals. Moreover, I also wish to understand from where I found the guts to face them, and how in this world I'm killing them...* he pondered.

Well, I can easily ask the detective. Certainly, I don't use any guns because I never owned one. Dave started to walk the street frantically.

He had to reach the Police Department in time for the appointment, but he also needed some answers to his questions.

Based on that information, he thought he might have planned a way to discover who he was-the shy editor with a gray existence, or a superhero capable of incredible acts.

It was hard to believe he was even thinking about this possibility.

This is absolutely inconceivable. I'm definitely not a killer; I refuse to think about something similar.

I might enjoy trying out the outfit when I'm home and impersonating my character, but this doesn't mean I'm the killer.

They got the wrong man, and it's all the fault of that stupid rumor my neighbors spread around of me being the avenger.

Flaring his nostrils, anger took over his reason. For the umpteenth time, he was in trouble because of other people.

He was once again played for a fool, simply because it was convenient, funny, and because he didn't react with the same anger as many others would.

"I'll never learn..." he chewed between his teeth.

He'd never reach the Police Department in time and looking around, he spotted a taxi, waving his hand to grab the attention of the driver.

As he got inside the car, he handed him the address. He won't have any difficulty in finding it; that's a sort of landmark.

His face upturned as he arrived in a timely manner at the destination, and rushing the speed of his steps, after one hour since his telephone call with Detective Orwell, he reached the hall.

"You're perfectly on time; I bet I could synchronize my clock with your precision," Kane greeted.

"Thanks, I was afraid I wouldn't make it. All sorts of incidents prevented me from being on time. But let's not talk about it. Here is the pen I used for the drawing; I didn't change the ink, so the results must be accurate."

"Well, we can't put an exact date on the drawing, but we can say whether it happened before or after Ms. Burroughs' arrival to your building. I guess this is also the time when this mysterious guy appeared," Placing a hand on his shoulder, Kane guided him to the lab. "I asked the analyst about what she would need for the analysis, and she confirmed a small sample of the ink would be enough to reach the result. This means that you don't need to buy another pen to use for the time needed to obtain the results."

Dave glanced at him, furrowing his brows. "Will it take a long time?"

"Well, at least one week, being positive, but it might also take more time if no final outcome is reached. But don't you worry, you won't be deprived of your drawing tools." Kane turned the pen between his fingers. "Is this so expensive?"

Dave smiled. "Well, this one was $70; the whole set was over $300."

"For one pen? I understand why you seemed to be so possessive of it!"

"Well, I don't spend money on vacations. I don't take free time from work. I don't have many friends and, most of all, I don't have a girlfriend, so my life is quite cheap if we want to put it from an economic perspective."

As soon as they reached the lab, they were greeted by Linda, who was expecting them. With a shy nod, Dave glanced at her.

"Hi."

"Good afternoon. So, this is the famous pen with which the drawing was made?" she asked.

"Yes." He blushed, due to the emphasis he put on how he needed to have it back. *I guess today is the day when I go and buy a whole set, even if I have to quit eating until the end of the month,* he thought.

"Well, come with me and let's get a sample of the ink, then you will only have to have patience and wait as we deliver the results," Jenna walked toward a counter.

As the samples were taken and Dave got back his pen, Kane guided him to the exit.

He had been observing him since the beginning and it wasn't necessary to be a detective to understand something was bothering him. "Is there anything wrong?"

"What?" Startled, as if his concerns were written all over his face, Dave turned his glance at him.

"Did anything happen to you?"

"No, I... I had a long morning, and I have so many thoughts in my head and I'm wondering how can I put them in order and find some peace? The latest events have turned my whole life upside down, and I'm trying to understand how to cope with them. Within a couple of months, I have found a friend, I experienced her missing, probably kidnapped by a stalker who was following her for a long time. I have been accused of murder, and because of it, I have lost my job... Okay, not really, but this period of forced vacation is an unfair punishment."

Shaking his head, Dave hoped to find a good excuse for his evident state of turmoil.

"I understand, and of course it's normal to feel stressed and confused. Yet, it seemed to me like something is scaring you. Did you receive any sort of threat? Did someone threaten you?"

"No, why do you think that?" Dave shook his head nervously as his heartbeat started to race. Never, more than at that moment, did he wish he could run away from one place.

His eyes glancing at the exit, figuring out a reasonable excuse to leave as fast as possible, he thought his heart would finally stop when he sensed the touch of Kane's finger on his neck.

"It's still bleeding a bit..." Kane leaned closer to scrutinize the cut made by the thug's knife.

"Oh... that was an accident when I shaved... just before coming here." His voice flickered.

"Of course," Kane couldn't believe the story.

This is not the cut of a razor. He knew Dave was hiding something, but he decided not to push it.

He was sure he would find out one day when every piece of the puzzle would finally be in their place. *I'm sure I'll also find a place in that picture for that wound, and not as a shaving accident.* "Well, I'll keep you informed about the investigation. In the meantime, I hope your life will become simpler than it has been in these past couple of months."

"Thank you very much, I appreciate your efforts. I'll be waiting for any news," Dave tried to calm down.

On his way to leave, he turned back to him. "One more thing, though."

"What would that be?" Kane tilted his head to one side.

"About those murders for which I was also suspected. How were those people killed? I must admit I wasn't informed about the weapon used by the killer, and as I was walking here, I started to think about it. Was it always the same one?" Kane glanced at him, surprised by his question.

He was sure if someone had been arrested for murder, he would have been updated about the crime he was suspected of.

"All the victims were found killed by stabbing; however, you can surely find all you need online. You will find a public statement by the police about the case, so you'd better find your information there..." Kane replied evasively.

"Any details about the possible weapon? Whether it was a kitchen, camping, or a combat knife?" Dave pursued.

"Why are you asking?"

"As you might know, last night another man was killed, and after your call, I started to consider that despite those crimes happening in my neighborhood, I had never thought about getting more details about it.

"To be honest I was focused on finding Gloria and defending myself from all sorts of accusations. However, now I'm starting to wonder about these murders too," Dave explained, hoping this didn't mean he might have been the killer.

He was aiming to know something more if he could find a similar weapon in his home, trying to figure out if it was so and he was the serial killer, or it was an instance of mistaken identity.

Knowing the weapon would have brought him to understand whether it could have been him who was the murderer or not.

Kane shook his head. "You'd better find it all on the net. I'm not investigating the case, so I can't give any information about it. I'm sorry."

"No, I get you. Mine was curiosity. I'll do as you suggested and find my answers from other sources." Dave left, still trembling from what had happened.

All he wanted at the moment was to erase everything from the day he met Gloria. "She has been like the Sun in my life, but I should have enjoyed her light from afar; now I got burned with all her problems. I wish I could do something more than waiting for Detective Orwell to solve the case. I need to find her, or at least to know she's fine," he pleaded aloud as he walked the streets. "After all, she has been the only friend I've had so far."

Then he recalled Alan invited him to join him at the bowling alley. *I'm not sure why he asked me, but maybe what I need now is to forget about my problems. Perhaps this is what I need, some social life.*

Glancing at his watch, he grimaced. "He said he'll be at the bowling alley within three hours, so I guess it gives me time to return home and do what I couldn't do before going to the Police Department. I hope I won't find anyone ready to kill me."

Despite his efforts in keeping himself busy, time seemed determined to stay still, and that gave Dave the idea of searching for some more information about the murders.

Particularly some details about the murder weapon, but perhaps he could first search his house and find out whether a knife, besides the ridiculous collection of knives he had, could be found as a confirmation of his suspicions.

"Well, this shouldn't be a difficult task. This apartment is rather small; moreover, I don't have many possessions, as I live quite a humble life. So perhaps searching the house will be faster than searching the internet," he considered looking through the kitchen.

Every sort of knife he found in his apartment was placed on the kitchen table as a comparison with the description of the murder weapon he obtained on the web.

Exploring every hidden corner, he found only three knives, one for the meat, one for the fish, and the other for the vegetables. In the living room, he even searched between the cushions of the couch, under the carpet, and behind the television.

Every cranny was explored, but nothing was found there.

The same situation applied to the bathroom and the walk-in closet. With a sigh, he reached the bedroom, which was the place that scared him the most, as it was also the place where the coat and the fedora were.

He glanced at the clock. "I won't have time to explore the bedroom now. I'll have to move the search until tomorrow morning or as soon as I come back from the bowling alley, depending on the time. At least, so far, I can consider my situation promising. Without a murder weapon, there can't be any chance that it's me who the killer is."

Relieved about it and with a smile on his face, he grabbed his jacket and left the building.

CHAPTER 11

The Christmas holidays went on without any significant events or news.

Also, since Dave couldn't find any trace of the murder weapon in his apartment, he started to regain his confidence in not being a freak, splitting his personality between his usual self and the brave avenger.

The comfort of having regained his life and identity, the certainty that he wasn't a psychopath who transformed himself into a ruthless assassin, returned his life to a quiet routine.

He never asked to be a superhero, especially if this meant having his life in danger.

Despite the need for a social life, he met with Alan only a couple of times before he left for the holidays until the second week of January.

Admittedly, having a friend to talk to was far better than his usual gray loneliness.

Nevertheless, spending his free time alone was not something new for him; he was used to it.

With Officer Orwell out of the city to follow a lead on Gloria's actual location, Dave felt lonely in a way he never thought he would.

For the sake of his mental health, he kept his television switched off, living only for his drawings, creating heroes and villains to become his best friends until someone returned from their holiday and the crazy period ended.

Jogging in the park became more frequent; besides being an activity he enjoyed and keeping himself busy, there he could meet some random walker or jogger, or he could find a pretty place to relax and enjoy nature.

During the same time frame, the criminals took a small break, and with them, the avenger disappeared once again in the mist and nobody heard about him anymore.

"I'm wondering whether by the time I return to work, my social life will change. At the moment, the biggest improvement I can hope for is to be left in peace without the bullying coming from my colleagues," Dave panted, ready to come back home from his daily jogging.

The ringing of his phone detached him from his thoughts.

"Stanford," he answered, coming inside his apartment.

"Good afternoon, this is Detective Orwell. Am I disturbing you?" Kane wondered.

Slipping his shoes off, Dave tried to keep his balance as he spoke. "No, I just returned from jogging. Do you have any news about Gloria?"

"Yes, I do. I followed her possible moves and, since the day she moved away from the apartment next to yours, she kept moving almost constantly. It seems clear to me she didn't consider it safe enough to rent a place anymore, and she booked rooms in motels, staying there for the maximum period of a couple of weeks. However, what's strange to me is how she didn't move far from the city. It's like she's circling around it," Kane explained, keeping his eyes at one particular motel, following a lead according to which she spent some time there as a guest.

He was going to talk to the receptionist, but he wanted first to update Dave about the situation, and hopefully, he'd find Gloria quite soon, bringing an end to the search.

It wasn't the thirst that guided Dave to the fridge; a cold beer before a shower was an institution after jogging. "I'm not surprised, but I hoped sooner or later she decided to go to the police and ask for protection from the stalker. Running away didn't work, as this guy kept following her. Moreover, I'm wondering why she isn't fleeing to a farther destination; it feels like she wants to be found by this man," Dave considered, reaching the couch, sipping his beer.

"That's an interesting point of view and could lead to an uncharted path." Keeping his eyes at the entrance of the motel from the car on the other side of the road, he pondered. "It could be that she's working for him or something similar. Of course, before we know that, I would need to find her, which appears to be quite a challenging task."

"Where are you now?" Dave almost considered the possibility of meeting him and maybe being of help in the search.

"Why do you want to know?" "Because perhaps I can come to you and offer a couple of extra hands. Besides, here there's nothing for me to do and things are getting frustrating." His hands caressed the soft velvet fabric of the couch.

"Forget about it. This is not a game, and if you're bored, find yourself a better hobby than drawing. We don't know what the deal is between Ms. Burroughs and this mysterious stalker, or whether there is a connection between them and the murders in your neighborhood," Kane replied resolutely, hitting the steering wheel of the car with a clenched fist. "Stay away from the investigation and out of trouble, as obviously, you attract it like a bee to honey."

Pouting, Dave felt once again discarded and treated like an irresponsible brat. "I understand, but it's not a question of getting bored, I was offering a hand."

"I repeat, this isn't something that concerns you. Keep yourself busy with more pleasant issues, and don't ask to participate in the investigation; this will never happen, mostly for yours and Ms. Burroughs' safety. At the moment, we can only guess she could be involved in something else, but in effect, we can't tell how dangerous this can turn out for her. So, if you want to be useful to her and yourself, steer clear."

His tone turned almost threatening, and the veins on his temples started to pulse furiously, which happened every time something frustrated him, whether the behavior of a person or a difficult situation.

"Okay, I understand," Dave slumped his shoulders. "Keep me informed about any progress."

"Of course, as soon as there is any news to be shared with you, be reassured, you will be the first one to be called. Now, I need to leave you. There's a place I must check before dark. Take care!" He ended the conversation, placed the mobile phone in his pocket, and exited the car.

He glanced around to make sure he had a clear idea of the surroundings, and toughening his expression, paced toward the entrance.

A warm whiff of air scented with spiced aromas of orange and cinnamon reached his nostrils as he entered the lobby.

The background music and the warmth of that simple, yet cozy environment gave him the impression of a place with higher standards than a typical motel.

Wearing his best smile, he walked to the reception desk.

"Good morning," greeted the receptionist. "Do you need a room?"

"It depends. At the moment, I don't think so, but perhaps you can help me to answer a few questions," he showed his badge.

"Of... course..." She hesitated, squeezing in her shoulders.

"I need to understand whether you saw this girl." He slipped the picture of Gloria out from the pocket of his jacket and placed it on the desk.

She took the sheet of paper in her hand and focused on the details, struggling to remember if someone resembling the girl was there. "I think she was one of our guests. I believe I saw her a couple of days ago. Do you know her name?"

"Gloria, Gloria Burroughs."

"I'll take a look at the records," she turned toward the computer she had on her desk. "Hmm, no there isn't anyone with that name here, but I'm almost sure I saw her here as a guest."

"Do you always check your guests' ID?" he pursued, wondering whether she used a fake one.

Open-mouthed, she was almost paralyzed at that question. She was afraid whatever she said might cause some trouble for the manager.

"I'm not investigating any irregularity. I'm trying to find this girl, and if you can tell me the name under which she booked the room, I would be grateful," Kane reassured.

"As a rule, we do ask for an ID, but it happens many times our guests prefer not to give any credentials or a credit card, as they generally pay cash. Many people come here to rent a room for one night to have sex with a prostitute, or to spend time with a lover..." she tried to explain, averting her gaze from him.

"And for this reason, you turn a blind eye on these *'irregularities,'* don't you?" Kane chuckled sarcastically.

"I guess you can say something similar, but please, if you need to take any steps against the administration of this motel, make sure I don't get involved. I need this job."

The corners of her trembling lips arched downwards, forecasting the end of her employment history, as a prelude of a dark, uncertain period.

Kane smirked with a grimace, crossing his arms on his chest. "I won't at this time, because I must find the girl, but it might be possible someone else will come to inspect this policy. You surely understand prostitution isn't legal, and everybody who is favoring such business is liable..."

The receptionist was shaking, fearing she was already in trouble because of what she revealed. "So, are you going to tell me the name by which she registered herself? At least you should have asked for her name and surname if she didn't want to give her ID," Kane challenged.

"No, I didn't say she didn't give us any identification; what I mean is this isn't the one she used to check-in. Eventually, she provided a fake ID, which wasn't looked over," she explained.

"Is there any way to know which name she gave you? Do you take any copies of those documents given by the customers?"

"Sure, we do take photocopies, but I'll need some time to go through all the IDs. I believe I can answer you later today or tomorrow afternoon." A concerned frown darkened her expression, knowing that she'd have to take some extra time in the evening to go through all the people who checked in over the past three weeks.

Kane tried to smile. "In this case, I think I will return then, and let's hope you find what I'm looking for." *If only I had the chance to obtain a warrant within a couple of hours, I could walk out of this motel with a copy of those names in a memory stick. Fuck the stupid bureaucracy!*

Kane pursed his lips as he turned his back, ready to leave.

"Would you like to take a room here? This way, as soon as I find her, I can call you. Don't you worry, you will be our guest, and I can give you our best room." She called him back, hoping to make up for the trouble caused by the administration.

Turning toward her, Kane considered the possibility. The place was pleasant enough, and he needed a place to stay anyway.

"Sure, you know how to do business. Well, you're right. If I'm here, I can be more easily in touch with you."

She smiled and handed him the form to be filled out for the check-in. "I'll also need your ID." She winked.

The room they gave him was indeed what he could believe was the best they had. He had no idea about the rates for their rooms, but at least the one he got was clean and the scent of fresh linen and winter spices relaxed his face into a smile.

He slipped his jacket and shoes off and toured the room. "That's not what I would call a motel. I'm sure this is something that goes beyond that definition."

***

In the darkness and stillness of the room, the ringing of the telephone startled him, ripping the thin curtain of his sleep.

Struggling to reach the light switch and get some sense about where he was and what was going on, he finally grabbed the insistent device.

"Hello," he mumbled groggily.

"Detective Orwell, I hope I'm not disturbing you, but I wanted to tell you that I have the ID of the girl. She registered herself under the name of Samantha Lewis." The victorious voice arrived at him like the sound of church bells on a bright summer morning.

"Hold on a second, what time is it?" With a loud yawn he searched for his mobile phone.

Blushing, she hesitated, hoping she didn't wake him up too early. "It's seven o'clock." Her voice lowered in tone.

"Damn! Either my alarm clock didn't ring, or I've overslept," Kane considered. "I'll come downstairs ASAP. Thank you."

He stood from the bed, still trying to understand where he was, and the best way was a cold shower. After about ten minutes, he was at the reception desk, eager to listen to what the receptionist had found.

"So, she registered under a different name? Can you give me a copy of her ID? I might want to check it out in case she had been seen somewhere else using the same credentials."

"Of course," she replied, sending the document to the printer.

Kane looked at the picture. Indeed, this is the same person. I wonder where she obtained such a well-made fake ID, he thought. There must be a lot to discover about this girl, and I'm going to find it out, even if I need to search for the rest of my life. "Well, thank you. I think I'll take this to the Police Department and start searching from there. When did she leave?" Kane wondered, glancing at the receptionist.

"She checked out two days ago, on Tuesday."

Considering what to do next and how he could trace her next move, he hesitated for a moment, caressing the smooth surface of the desk. "I wonder whether she's still in the city, or if she moved away. Did she come in a car or a taxi?"

"She came in a cab, as she asked me to call one to reach the station. She left at noon." That was a detail she was also surprised to recall.

Generally, she never cared about how the customers reached the motel. It was, perhaps, because the driver helped her to bring the suitcase inside the lobby.

A guest arrived from his room, handing the key for the day to the receptionist. A swift smile appeared on her face as she wished him a good day.

"And do you always rely on a particular company?" Kane pursued, waiting for the customer to leave the lobby.

"Yes, we do. Here is the business card for the taxi service we use. Perhaps by asking them, you might find out who picked up the girl and where she asked to go." Glancing at the card, a satisfied smile appeared on his face, with the sensation of being close to the solution of the case.

"That's exactly what I'm going to do. This is the key to the room. Thank you for the hospitality and have a great day!" he blurted, pacing away.

"Thanks, and good luck!" she watched him exiting the lobby.

However, as he reached the door, he hesitated and turned his gaze to the girl who was already back to caring about her own business.

Recalling the presence of the fedora man, he thought he could ask the receptionist about him. "Oh, I almost forgot about it. Did you notice anything strange about her? For example, did she look like she was nervous or worried about anything?"

"No, she was always smiling. I don't think she had any trouble. You know, the typical person who's here for a vacation and is enjoying her time."

"Did anyone come to visit while she was here? Any telephone calls?" Kane pursued, starting to get excited by the direction of that chat.

"No, as far as I'm concerned, she was always alone. She used to go out in the morning to return in the evening after dark. I can't say what she was doing during the day, though."

"And did you see anyone walking around here who caught your attention? Perhaps someone with a peculiar way of dressing." At that question, she remained silent for a moment to think about it.

There were a lot of people coming and going, particularly visiting the guests, so it wasn't an easy task to recall whether a particular guest used to have any visitors.

But then she shook her head. "No, nobody who attracted my attention in any special way, at least from my point of view."

"How long did she stay in this motel?"

"She was here for about three weeks, which was one of the longest stays we've recorded," she giggled, amused.

"Did she ever ask for a restaurant or any other place?"

"No, I had the impression that she knew the town and returned after a long absence. She wasn't the kind of person who needed any guidance about the place, but on the other hand, nowadays the internet replaced tourist info agencies, and people can find all sorts of information from their mobile phones."

Kane nodded. "How did she pay for the hotel room?"

"Hold on, I'm going to check it," she averted her glance to look at the screen of the computer.

"She paid with a credit card."

"I need the details of it," he said.

"You'll need a warrant," she whispered, leaning toward him with a cunning smile arching the corners of her mouth.

"Do I have to remind you that you're hosting an illegal activity connected to the exploitation of prostitution?" His expression toughened, hating being contradicted.

Narrowing her eyes, she grimaced, challenging him but understanding her weaker position, her lips pursed together into a pout. "I'll print it immediately for you," she huffed.

"Wise decision!" As Kane got the printed sheet of the transaction, one thing caught his attention. "The name on the card and the one on the ID don't match!" he exclaimed.

"I-I paid no attention to that detail..." she cooed, embarrassed. "You didn't? This is enough to call the police right away! What if it was stolen, and she had a fake ID?" Kane yelled, slamming his hand on the desk.

She blushed, understanding how she'd acted carelessly, and walked a couple of steps backward, shaking at the way the manager would shout at her before kicking her out of the place.

With a long exhale, he brought his hand to his forehead.

He scanned the whole transaction which was still approved by the bank. "I'm sorry, I lost my temper. This means she had a fake ID, and this brings me to another level of consideration."

He remained for a moment, thinking about what to do next, and the first thing that came to his mind was to get the name of the taxi company to obtain the needed information about her next move. "For now, I don't have any other questions for you, so I will go and continue my search," he glanced at her.

"Take care!"

"Thanks, the same to you," she replied in a whisper. As Kane walked back to his car, he took out his mobile phone and immediately called the taxi company and asked for their local headquarters.

Talking to someone at the call center won't help. I need more detailed information, he considered with a grin on his face. When he got the address, he steered his car in the direction of the main office. She's two days ahead of me, but luck might be on my side.

Entering the premises of the taxi dispatch center, he paced confidently toward the info desk, and without taking time to glance around at the environment, he asked to talk with the manager, certain he was the only one who could give him the information he was looking for. "I admit this is a surprise for me. Having a police officer in my office searching for a missing girl is quite rare. I hope I can help you find this person" Mrs. Rainer smiled, inviting him to take a seat.

"Thank you, so do I," he slipped out from the pocket of his jacket the copy of the ID he received from the motel.

The quality of the picture was better than the one he had already. "This is the girl who asked for a taxi from the Dreamtime Motel." Kane handed her the photograph of the girl. "According to the receptionist, she left on Tuesday at noon, so three days ago."

Mrs. Rainer glanced at the image on the ID and turned to the computer. "I'll check who took the call. I guess the driver should remember where she asked to be driven."

"Here!" she exclaimed. "Mr. Thompson was the one, and his car is still here, so he must be around. I will ask him to come in here." With a swift move, she grabbed the phone.

Knowing an officer was waiting for him didn't sound like good news at all for Mr. Thompson, and after about five minutes, he hesitatingly knocked at the door, gingerly peeking from the opening when invited to come in.

"Mr. Thompson, this is Detective Orwell," Mrs. Rainer commenced, inviting him to come inside. "He's here because three days ago you picked up a girl from the Dreamtime Motel at noon. Do you remember anything about her?"

Drawing a deep breath, he was relieved to understand he was not in trouble and the question was only about a customer he had.

Nevertheless, he answered many calls from that place and forced his mind to focus on that particular day. "Several times a day, I'm called to pick up one of the guests; can you give me more details about the girl?"

"Of course. Here is a picture of her." She handed him a copy of the ID. "Oh, yes, I remember her." He nodded confidently, after a fast glance at the image. "She asked me to bring her to the main station. That's the place where most of the people I pick up from that motel are going."

"Did she pay with a credit card?" he asked, squeezing his thumb inside his fist until it hurt.

"She paid with cash. In my cab, I haven't yet installed the system for the card payment."

"Hmm, this makes it almost impossible to trace her position now, particularly because she used a fake ID," Kane growled. "Did you ask her where she was going to?"

"No, she didn't seem like a person who wanted to talk with the driver. When you do this kind of work, you can immediately recognize the type who's looking for a chat from the other who prefers to keep the relationship strictly professional. That's the reason why I didn't even ask," Mr. Thompson explained.

"Do you think she was in a particular state of mind? I mean, was she worried, in a hurry, relaxed?"

"She was calm, and she didn't look agitated or concerned about anything that raised my attention. She looked like the regular tourist who is going back home after a relaxing holiday," Mr. Thompson glanced nervously at his supervisor as if to find a friendly face.

Kane remained for a moment to think about his next move or the next question he needed to ask, but rather than getting closer to her, she'd slipped once again from his hands like a wriggling fish.

With a twitch of his mouth, he stood from his chair. "For the moment, I don't need anything else. Thank you very much for your cooperation. I think I'll have to find out a way to track this girl's position."

"I hope you will find her soon," Mrs. Rainer replied.

When Kane was finally back on the street, he sighed. "She's no longer missing, so the case is closed. It's suspicious that she keeps moving from place to place, not to mention the fact that she used a fake ID. This, however, falls outside the scope of the search. If she's caught up in illegal activity, we might reopen a file on her, but I need to discuss it with the Lieutenant, and that's precisely what I'm going to do as soon as I finish with my report.

"In terms of the actual missing person investigation, the case is closed, and I'll have to inform Mr. Stanford about what I've found, so if he wants to find this girl, he has to do it on his own." He returned to his car, ready to go back to his office at the Police Department to file a report about the case and archive it.

When he was inside, he grabbed his phone and called Dave.

"Stanford," he answered, as he was going to the park for his daily jogging.

"Good morning, this is Detective Orwell. Am I disturbing you?"

"Good morning. No, you're not. Nowadays there is no way to disturb me, at least until I can go on and get my job back or get a new one," Dave smiled, opening the door of his apartment, ready to leave.

"I called you to say we're closing the search for Gloria Burroughs. She was here three days ago at a motel about 70 miles away from the city. She then moved away somewhere else using the train. Since the requirement for a person to be missing is that nobody has seen her, or she has been seen in difficult situations, are not fulfilled, we need to consider the case closed," Kane explained, expecting Dave to protest about his decision. *I don't make the rules. If a girl is going away with a train, she isn't missing; she left.*

"But she might still be in danger." He hesitated on the first flight of stairs, turning his glance at the apartment where she used to live.

"Potentially, we all are, but this doesn't mean we all need to be rescued from something, which is unlikely to happen. Ms. Gloria Burroughs hasn't been abducted. She might have left the house because a stalker threatened her, but this is, again, conjecture. We do not have any evidence of it, besides the fact that the same man appeared in two of the places where she lived. From my point of view, someone stalked her, but Ms. Burroughs handled the situation on her own. She's free to go to the Police Station and ask for help, and perhaps one day that's what she'll do. Yet, the case for a missing person is closed."

Dave thought about it for a moment, and he had to admit he was right, and the police had too many cases on their hands to take care of everybody who potentially might have been in trouble. "I understand, and you're probably right when you say she might no longer be missing, though I miss her and wish to meet her again," Dave considered.

"Perhaps she wanted to be far from you too, or she didn't want to involve you in her problems." A deep exhale escaped Kane's mouth.

"Yeah, well, I'm grateful for your help, and I'm glad to know that at least she's still alive and not kidnapped by any sort of psychopath. She didn't have any intention of keeping in contact with me, and that's all. I thought... Oh, well, never mind." He lowered his gaze and started to climb down the stairs, determined to forget about her the same way she did with him.

That shouldn't have been anything new for a gray person like him.

He'd never felt connected with anyone else in the world the way he felt with her. "Don't take it too seriously. She's not the only girl in this world," Kane said. "But now I need to go, and I'll have to file a final report about this case. By the way, how are you doing today?"

That question unsettled him, forcing his expression to freeze into a grimace. "What do you mean?"

"Well, last time you were at the Police Department, I had the impression that something or someone was after you," Kane clarified.

The way those murders appeared to swirl around Dave and this mysterious Gloria Burroughs intrigued him.

A nagging voice in the back of his head kept yelling about a connection between them, and if he looked carefully, he would solve the whole case.

Yet, with still too many pieces missing in that puzzle, he needed to plan what to do next with his direct supervisor. "Oh, yes, sure. Well, as I explained to you the last time, the recent events in my life shook me a bit, and I'll require some time to adjust myself to it. Now, as you mention it, at least one of the problems which kept me awake at night had been solved, so I can start to focus on my life. I guess the case of the mysterious serial killer, who had murdered a few of the local criminals is still open, but since it's clear I'm not involved, I should stop thinking about it. Then at the end of next month, I'll go back to work, and everything should finally return to the usual routine." That was at least what he hoped.

"I guess you're right, and I wish you all the best for the future. However, with your talent, if you find yourself without a job, you might consider the career of a sketch artist for the Police Department."

"Thanks, I'll keep that in mind," Dave chuckled. "Have a nice day."

As he ended the conversation, Dave shook his head.

I thought she liked me, but perhaps Detective Orwell is right, and women are mysterious creatures. Now that I know she's alive and well, I can concentrate on my own life, and I'll start with a good jog. Today I want to go over my record, maybe this way I can get so tired that even thinking will be hard to achieve.

***

As the days went by, Dave could hardly acknowledge the passage of time.

Since he was threatened on the street, he kept himself mostly inside his apartment. He decided it wasn't safe to show his face outside.

Perhaps he also started to become paranoid but being mistaken for the avenger was something he didn't need in his life.

"It's one thing to be admired as the mysterious superhero by the kids around this neighborhood; it's another thing to be considered as such by those who have been threatened by this guy." Dave shook his head as he was drawing one of his superheroes.

"I wish I had at least some superpowers, so I could face them on equal terms. I'm also wondering whether it would be wiser for me to search for another apartment to rent. If I move away from this place, they will finally leave me be and I'll be able to continue my life the way it used to be before all this craziness started." He opened up the computer, searching for deals on rental apartments somewhere else.

"Hmm, what if they fire me? Perhaps I should wait until my vacation is over before even considering moving." He stood from the chair, grabbed by the fear of remaining unemployed. "What will become of me if I lose my job? How am I going to pay the rent and other expenses? I'll end up homeless!" He gasped for air, thinking of having no place to live.

For him, life happened mostly between the safety of the four walls of his apartment. He had no idea what would happen to him if he had to defend himself on the streets.

His life started to jump from one problem to another, and he couldn't see any peace happening soon. "Well, this isn't something new. I was so distracted by all the other issues that I didn't for a second stop to think about it. I should have thought about it, and maybe now it's the time to act," he sat on the chair of his computer's desk.

Instead of searching for a new apartment, it's better to search for new employment, and perhaps, as Detective Orwell suggested, I might send a resume as a sketch artist. If I'm lucky, they might need a new one soon, and I might get the chance to find a job right away. Thinking about it, I'm not eager to return to my old job. That's something I can do if there won't be any other alternative, but I'm not going to like it the way I used to, he thought.

He started to browse the job offers, without a clear idea of whether he should search for new employment as an artist or editor. "I guess it's easier to find a job as an editor since it was my profession for the last ten years. At least I'm not missing experience in the field."

CHAPTER 12

Gloria reached the hotel room after she checked in. The click of the door closing on its hinges coincided with the ringing of her mobile phone, as if they were linked together.

Perfect timing! She thought.

She didn't need to look at the caller ID. "I was waiting for your call." Gloria walked to the window, glancing at the street from behind the curtains.

"Are you already in the hotel?" The gravelly, rushed voice of Anton reached her ears, enhancing the apprehension coursing through her veins since she'd left.

"Yes, can you give me any news about James?" She moved away from the window and sat down on her bed, testing the softness of the mattress.

"The detective who searched for you finally archived the case, so there isn't anyone nosing around in our business anymore. Concerning James, we have solid grounds to believe he's starting to recall everything. We must intervene as soon as possible and bring him back to his duties." A slight pause allowed her to reconsider the whole situation.

She doubted the time for him to remember everything had arrived. "Do you think he's ready to come back into service?"

"We will see. The most important thing now is to get him back. His real self is emerging from the induced state we put him in, and I'm afraid if we don't act soon, someone is going to kill him. What's your impression of him?"

"Personally, I hoped we could bring him back since last year. I understand Doc didn't share my same opinion and wanted to be cautious, but after what I saw, I guess it's a good idea. I'm also starting to miss him." A deep exhale betrayed her state of mind.

"Trust me, he's missing you too, whether he realized it or not. Giving him back that particular drawing was a good move. I believe he started to recall at a conscious level something about the past we temporarily erased."

The memory of the past times spent together brought a shy smile to her face. However, the first reaction experienced by the few other members who needed the same treatment provided her a valid reason to fear for the future of their relationship.

"Well, it wasn't supposed to be a permanent solution. What I'm concerned about will be his response. Are we going to explain to him his identity?"

"This is what we will do, and perhaps you should also be there."

"When will this happen?" She stood from the bed, nervously pacing around the room.

"Before he murders someone else and the gangs keep their promise and retaliate against him; I'm afraid this might occur quite soon, unfortunately." Anton tried to maintain a calm tone of voice.

"Is there anyone who is watching over him?"

"As usual," Anton assured, "he has never been left alone for one second. As in the beginning, we had followed him to keep track of his moves and mental recovery. Now we need to look after him and his safety. We got to bring him back alive."

"So, do you think I should reach the headquarters?" Gloria wondered.

"James' reintegration is our priority, so I would say you should return right away, but make sure nobody is following you. For how many days did you book the hotel room?"

"I kept my check-out date flexible. I can move this moment if required. They know already I might be here for a period between one day or one month. Don't you think it would be better to stay here for more than a day? I know there isn't anyone following me, but I still would like to play it safe."

"I agree." Anton nodded thoughtfully. "However, I want you to understand that it's a foggy day, and, well, our mysterious avenger gets overexcited on nights like this."

Gloria giggled. "Take good care of both."

"We always do our best, and you know it. Tomorrow afternoon, you will check out and return to the headquarters. We're now planning a way to bring James back in. Doc will worry about the rest."

Her glance met her image in the mirror; the light frown revealed a turmoil not even her perfect smile could conceal. "Brilliant, I'll inform the receptionist and will start preparing myself to be there in the evening. See you then, and whatever happens, keep me informed."

"Be reassured about it. Bye." As soon as Anton ended the conversation, Gloria averted her gaze from the mirror.

Too many open issues required her focus before leaving. Pursing her lips, she tried to make a sort of list of duties for the day.

First, I'll go downstairs to the reception desk and inform them about the time of my checkout. Then I'll need to arrange the fastest way to reach the headquarters for tomorrow evening, she thought. I can't wait to have him back. Those five years felt like an eternity, and although we had him under strict surveillance, the distance seemed overwhelming. My only hope is our lives will return to be the way they used to be.

Without lingering, she reached the reception desk. "I got a call from my supervisor and I must leave tomorrow afternoon. Can I pay the fee now to avoid wasting time then?" she asked the receptionist, handing him the key to the room, as she was ready to go out to arrange her transportation.

The man at the desk grabbed the key and smiled kindly. "Of course. Hold on a second and I'll prepare the receipt. Will you check out before or after 10 am?"

"I'd prefer a later checkout. I need to take care of other issues during the morning." She turned her gaze toward the door as someone entered the hall.

"Then, I must charge half of the daily fee for tomorrow, and it's going to be $180.00, please."

With a contained smile, hoping to hide the euphoric excitement coursing through her body, she opened her purse to get the card.

As she left the hotel, she scanned the surrounding environment, trying to spot anyone who might be following her.

Being sure she hadn't been followed, she walked the streets, thinking about the best way to leave. *I guess the fastest route would be either renting a car or the train. Buses are always the least reliable means of transportation, and taxis... well, I'm not interested in giving the address of the headquarters to anyone in this world*, she considered, as she walked to the metro station to reach the central railway station.

There she could get both the train's schedule and the car rental fare, so she would have everything ready for the following day.

Waiting for the train on the subway, her thoughts returned to James, recalling the time they'd spent together and the nervous breakdown that forced the organization to make the decision to temporarily suspend him from his duties.

Those methods might appear extreme to any outsider, but the problem required drastic measures to avoid having him locked away in a mental facility. Thinking about it, five years locked into a false identity was a better deal than an asylum. I hope he will recall this was something he agreed to. Generally, those who come back from that state maintain a sort of hostile attitude for at least a year. On the bright side, after that, everyone who went through it recovered fully and was reintegrated into the original tasks. I just hope we will be able to go on with our relationship. I'm not expecting it to be the same as it was. Actually, I wish to have it improved.

With a sigh, she stepped into the train. Once again, she glanced around, scrutinizing every person already inside and those who came in with her.

Without caring, and immersed in her thoughts, she reached the central railway station, where she could compare the timetable with the time it would take to drive a car to the headquarters.

Hmm... the difference isn't so big, but perhaps with a car, I'll have more freedom to change my route if the situation requires it.

She frowned as she scanned the train's timetables. It took a few minutes to consider what would be the best choice and despite it all, she preferred taking a car from the rental services.

***

The night he'd spent drawing new stories and characters, inspired by the avenger and the concept of a brand-new superhero, and gave him a new routine.

In the morning, opening his eyes didn't seem to fit with what his body planned. Turning a few times, lingering wrapped in the sheets felt like a better idea than waking up, and if it wasn't for his plan to go jogging a bit earlier, he would have remained in his bed for a longer time.

With a loud yawn, Dave stood from the bed and went to open the windows to let some fresh air in. "Well, more than that, I would call it freshly polluted, but I would consider it more oxygenated than the air in this room," he chuckled.

After a shower, he sat once again at the table where he used to draw and took a look at what he'd been sketching the previous night.

Apparently, this Humphrey Bogart man, together with the tale of the avenger has been of great inspiration to my drawings.

This is the kind of hero everybody wished to have in their neighborhood, and perhaps I should also start to write storylines for my character. I suppose he needs to go into action.

The sirens of the police and an ambulance distracted him from his considerations, and since it sounded like they were coming in his direction, he hurried to check what had happened.

As he reached the window of his bedroom, he spotted the paramedics bringing a couple of corpses out from the building in front of the one where he was living.

They were covered, but he understood what was underneath the coverings. One thing he was afraid of was that if any of those bodies belonged to any of the members of the gangs, his life could be in dire danger.

He still trembled at the threat he received when he was going to the Police Department, and it seemed to be darn serious.

Having his senses heightened by the adrenaline rush, he closed the window and withdrew a couple of steps away from it.

His heart started to pound in his chest. "If this is the act of the mysterious avenger, I'm fucked!" he breathed, thinking of where to hide, or whether he should call the police asking for protection.

Frantically, he glanced around trying to find a makeshift weapon to defend himself in case they came to kill him, but the most dangerous weapon he could find in his apartment was either one of the kitchen knives or a cast iron pan.

"I should call the police... I should call Detective Orwell and explain to him the situation. I need protection and I need it now, or tomorrow the next victim is going to be me," he considered as his voice started to tremble.

He locked the front door and went to see how many days he could afford to live without going for groceries or leaving the house. "I can manage to survive for a week, but I doubt they're in a hurry to get me. Most likely they're already planning a way to reach my apartment. They could enter by the windows, and at that point, there wouldn't be anyone able to save me."

Tears started to flow from his eyes as he grabbed the phone to reach out to the last hope he had.

"Detective Orwell," Kane answered in a busy tone.

"G-Good morning, Officer, this is Dave Stanford. Did I call you at a bad moment?" His voice flickered.

"Mr. Stanford, this is a surprise. And no, you didn't disturb me, but did anything happen? You sound scared."

"I am, too," he whined with the last breath he had. "Last night, there was again a murder in my neighborhood, and I was wondering whether you can give me any details about it."

"Until it comes out in the newspaper, all information is classified, and I'm not allowed to reveal anything about it."

"I know, but this is a question of life and death, particularly mine," Dave tried to explain.

"Something you need to know is that, for some reason I ignore, people in my building started to believe I am the mysterious avenger, and this is obviously some sort of conviction which makes them feel safe.

However, it puts me in a difficult position, as those rumors also arrived to the ears of those gangs whose members were murdered. Recently, one of them threatened me, warning me not to intervene anymore in their business. Of course, I'm not involved in this mess, and I'm afraid they'll be after me as soon as the police retrieve the bodies and secure the crime scene. Please, Officer, I desperately need help." Kane remained silent for a moment, considering what Dave was saying.

Recalling the nervous state he was in when he reached the Department the last time, and the small, fresh wound on his neck, everything started to make sense.

Whether someone was playing with his safety, taking advantage of the fact that everybody considered Dave the avenger, he had to act quickly.

"Mr. Stanford, why didn't you tell me earlier about this threat? You understand you could have been brought to a safe location as a witness?" He placed his mobile phone on the table and wiped his hair back with his hands.

The circumstances required quick action, and he wasn't sure there would be anything he could do fast enough to protect him, but he needed to try at least.

This was the best chance to get the whole situation solved. With a deep breath, he grabbed the phone once again. "Listen to me carefully. Do not exit your apartment for any reason. I'll send a couple of officers to get you from your apartment and take you to the Police Department. I guess this avenger is taking advantage of this rumor to act the way he wants. We will be there as soon as possible. When they leave, I will call you to inform you about their arrival and their names," Kane spoke slowly and calmly. "In any case, don't panic. Stay away from the windows and from the door." "I'll be waiting for your call." He tried to hide his emotional state and keep his voice steady, hanging up the conversation. His knees failed him, and he fell on the ground with a loud thump.

He couldn't grab a stable thought in the turmoil of his mind, wondering who would be the first to arrive – the gangsters or the police.

With the uncontrollable shaking taking over his body, he struggled to reach the couch. The door was already locked. Grabbing onto the arms of the sofa, he made it to stand on his feet.

As if he had just learned how to walk, he wobbled to lock the doors to those rooms whose windows were easily accessible from the street.

Then he remained to wait for a call, listening to his heartbeat and the noises coming from the other apartments.

A few minutes went by and his belly started to complain of its emptiness. Considering dying with a full stomach would have perhaps fulfilled his last wish, he walked to the kitchen to prepare coffee and some cereal with milk.

The stillness in the apartment and from the neighboring residences was so perfect, he thought they'd been evacuated.

Not even the usual noises coming from the corridor, or from the television his neighbor used to listen too loud was to be heard.

Dave felt like he'd been left alone in the whole world, together with those who, like wolves, waited in the darkness for any false move.

Time moved slowly, and he wondered whether the police would come and rescue him.

Every minute they were wasting was a minute closer to his death. Suddenly, in the most complete silence of his apartment, the ringing of his mobile phone echoed like the judgment's bells.

Jumping like a spring, Dave spilled the bowl of cereal on the floor as he stumbled over everything on his way to reach the telephone on the couch.

"Stanford," he gasped.

"You're dead," growled a voice, immediately ending the conversation.

Gasping for air, as if his heart had already jumped out of his chest, he felt he was going to die before they arrived.

They knew where he was, and they were coming for him to fulfill the promised punishment for a man they thought to be the bravest or the stupidest of them all.

"Where the fuck is the police?!" A whimper came out of his mouth.

He dialed once again the number of Detective Orwell, but there wasn't any signal to be reached with his phone. Releasing all the tension, his sobs and cries raised to reach almost the streets, or whoever could have some mercy even for a loser like him.

Death wasn't a welcome guest in his soul, not yet and not the way they promised, he thought, sniffing through his tears.

Frozen on the floor as if paralyzed by terror, he couldn't move or stand on his feet.

He feared that when the police arrived, they would have to break down the door to come inside; he was sure his body would refuse to respond to any order from his brain. "How the fuck did I get myself into this situation?" he whimpered, trembling and cuddling against the couch.

He remained on the floor, listening to every little noise coming either from the streets or from the building.

Questions about whether any of those gangsters knew precisely where his apartment was, filled his mind.

Therefore, he turned his phone to silent. "If they're going to call me to get my position, at least it won't ring as loudly as it did before." He then checked the signal and although it was restored, he wondered whether calling the police would put him in more significant danger. "Once upon a time with the landline phones, you would have never been traceable like with these stupid devices," he considered, grinning through his teeth.

He crawled to the kitchen to grab at least a knife. It won't solve my situation, but it might give me some extra time to call for help.

Although, I seriously doubt any of the people who live here will ever offer to put their lives in danger to save the avenger.

Suddenly the noise of footsteps resounded in the corridor, and he heard them coming closer and closer.

They reached the door, and someone knocked heavily at his door: "Police!" one of them yelled, "Mr. Stanford, open the door!"

With a euphoric, hysterical chuckle, the nightmare was finally over, and someone arrived to save him.

He would have preferred to face a life sentence in jail, even being accused unfairly of being the avenger rather than being caught by those gangsters.

He promptly stood from the ground, struggling to reach the door, but when he opened it, he found the two policemen lying on the floor.

Before he realized what was going on and the reason why they were dead, when just a second before they could have offered safety, a couple of guys grabbed him, promptly dragging him out of the apartment.

It was a question of seconds, and soon enough, he was gagged and restrained, regardless of all his efforts to wriggle from their grasps and run away.

"We've warned you, but you wanted to play the hero, didn't you?" one of them grinned, forcing him to his feet and whispering in his ear. He was so close his hair tickled Dave's neck.

Fear ran along his spine like the crawling of a thousand spiders. "Well, avenger, now try to save yourself. We're soon going to discover how many of your body parts need to be removed before you die." They both laughed, dragging him down the stairs to the street.

A light fog embedded the whole place like a cottony web, and for a moment, Dave thought about his man from the mist.

For once, he won't come to save me, regardless of whether it was he who put me into this situation. I wish I were a superhero and could kill those two guys, together with that asshole of an avenger, he cursed through his clenched teeth.

On the other side of the road, there was a black van with the back doors open. They yanked Dave across the street as he tried to struggle and break free from their grasp.

Feeling his legs failing him, probably he would have just fallen on the street, but everything was worth trying, and most of all he knew for sure he didn't want to come inside the van.

The two men managed to bring him to the van, ready to be lifted up.

"What the fuck is this?" yelled one of the two gangsters.

Dave couldn't see what he meant, as everything happened behind him, but whatever it was, they didn't like it.

Before anyone could react in any way, he was startled by several gunshots.

The blow was so close, he was almost sure they'd shot him, but although he dropped on the ground and his back was hurting, he was still alive.

He fell on the corpses of his captors. Whoever was in the van could become his best friend, unless he was one of the bosses who wanted to have the personal satisfaction of killing the avenger.

Without any words spoken, someone grabbed him from behind, and he didn't find the courage to face the ones who'd temporarily saved his life.

They dragged him to the van, and one of them closed the doors, bringing complete darkness around him. "You haven't lost your ability to get yourself into trouble, James," he heard someone finally speaking to him.

"Who the fuck is James? My name is Dave..." he protested as soon as he could regain his breath. Obviously, whoever kidnapped him didn't mean to kill him right away.

"Yeah, Dave Stanford... that name fits you, somehow," a deep, masculine voice sneered. As his heart began to slowly return to a regular pace, he was also confident about his voice being firm enough to speak.

"Who are you and where are you bringing me?" "You will know soon, but don't you worry, we're the good guys; we're friends," the same voice replied from an unspecified location in the darkness.

"Of whom? Certainly not mine; my friends would never drag me into a van, keeping me in the dark, and with my hands cuffed behind my back," Dave complained, as he tried to find a position that wouldn't hurt him.

The man laughed, amused. "You will be freed as soon as we arrive at the destination. There, we will explain everything. I believe you remember Gloria, don't you?"

"What the fuck have you done to her!" Dave yelled angrily. A deeper level of terror mixed with a furious rage possessed his soul.

"Whoa, cool down. She's waiting for you, and she's alive and well. Why would we do anything wrong to one of our best agents?"

At that point, nothing made any sense anymore, and he was almost sure he would soon wake up from what appeared to be a nightmare.

"A-agents? I don't understand."

"We will answer all your questions, but not yet, and not here." From that moment on, it seemed like Dave was alone, although he knew whoever was there with him couldn't have disappeared.

In the darkness, time lost any meaning and the only thing he could be sure of was that they left the paved road.

His back was already sore and his arms numb. Despite the discomfort he felt, he preferred not to say a word and wait to reach the destination they were driving him to.

Many questions started to populate his mind, but the most urgent was what did Gloria have to do with this story and those people? *Why did they call me James, and why did they say she's one of their agents? What did they mean? Do those people belong to a government organization, or are they independent? What do they do, and what do they want from me?*

After a whole eternity, the van finally stopped, and the doors opened. The bright daylight hit Dave's eyes, forcing him to close and open them many times before he was able to see anything.

When he could distinguish and recognize what he saw, he was indeed astounded to see, not merely the sky was no longer gray but blue, and the fog was gone.

Most of all, he was surprised when he saw the Humphrey Bogart guy standing close to him. *I was talking to Gloria's stalker all this time?*

Open-mouthed, his mind was suddenly blank, as if all the thoughts in his mind mixed up with one another in the utmost confusion.

"I can almost hear all your questions, James. I guess we will need some time to get through everything that happened in the last five years," the man in the coat and fedora beamed. "But let's remove those cuffs, and then let's go inside where you will have all your questions answered."

Dave didn't reply, being grateful to have those restraints, sending an unspeakable pain through all his body, removed.

He looked around, surprised about the place where he was.

The tall and large villa in front of which the van was parked seemed to bring back some memories, although they appeared to come from another life.

An old British Victorian-style mansion surrounded by an exceptionally manicured garden reminded him of old movies he'd seen sometimes on TV during his lazy days.

What came first in his mind at the view of such an imposing building was a dollhouse with elaborate trim, bright colors, and beautiful tiled roof.

The walls decorated with wooden frames offered him a glimpse of the style waiting for him inside, enriching its beauty.

Moreover, the location seemed to be quite far from any sort of civilization, and he wondered whether he was brought somewhere abroad.

He couldn't remember anything like that located in the surroundings of the city. Feeling the gentle touch of Humphrey Bogart's hand guiding him toward the villa gave him a reassuring sensation.

The man in the fedora hat walked silently at his side, trying to guess Dave's state of mind, wondering about the recovery process he would have to undergo.

Their jobs constantly put them under a high level of mental stress, and sometimes it happened that some of them went through a nervous breakdown.

The main door was open, and as they came in, Dave gasped.

If he was amazed by the exterior of that impressive building, he felt almost intimidated by its interior, and hesitated for a moment at the view of the hall.

Glancing around, there wasn't any chance for him to indulge and appreciate any of the particulars that made that place unique.

His eyes were grabbed alternately by the many subtle details. He raised his gaze to look at the ceiling, almost failing to find an end to those tall walls reaching the second story.

"We need to go," the deep voice of Humphrey Bogart resounded through the hall, and without any reply from Dave, they walked away.

The ticking of their steps on the expensive marble that covered the floor seemed to echo in the religious silence embedding the premises, as anticipation rose in Dave's soul.

None of them spoke a word until they finally reached a vast room, different from the rest of the house.

This one was simply furnished with a long desk on one side and a couple of couches on the other side.

Something he noticed that made his heart jump in his chest, was the presence of a woman he thought he'd lost forever – Gloria.

She opened up with a bright smile and ran to hug him. "I was so afraid we would arrive too late," she whispered, as his senses seemed to melt at the touch with her body and the scent of her perfume.

Dave held her tightly to himself, feeling her body close to his, relieving him of the stress he'd accumulated during that day.

It was obvious enough they were indeed friends, and they just saved his life. "When I saw your apartment empty, I feared I would never see you again. I trembled at the thought someone kidnapped you," he parted from her with the surreal feeling of having her so close, as he couldn't have ever imagined it possible.

Then he turned to face the other men in the room. "Now I guess it's the perfect time to explain to me what's going on. Most of all, why is this guy calling me James when my name is Dave?" His finger, pointing at the man with the fedora.

"Well, let me introduce myself, although there shouldn't be any reason, as we have been colleagues for at least ten years. My name is Anton Bélanger. You already know Gloria Burroughs, and this other man is Dr. Karl Nielsen," he removed his coat and hat. "Please have a seat. This is going to be a long explanation, and an even longer day is waiting for you, starting from now."

They all sat down on the couches, and Dr. Nielsen took over the speech, bringing the palms of his hands together in front of his mouth. "Your real name is James Eldings, and you're a special agent for a mercenary military organization called *The New Order*. Five years ago, during an operation, one of our agents was killed, and Gloria seriously injured. The problem behind this incident, which is part of the business anyway, was your liability."

"Wait a second!" Dave interrupted, standing up from the couch. "Are you telling me that I'm a sort of special forces' agent, and during an operation, because of me, one of us died? I can't even hold a gun! You're mistaking me with another man, like those who think I'm the avenger do!" He spread his arms apart, hoping he would wake up soon, because he started to fear the realism of that nightmare.

"No, we don't mistake you for another person, James; please sit down." Dr. Nielsen kept his voice quiet, locking his eyes on Dave. "Let me finish the story. We gave you some time to recover mentally from the shock, but nothing could help, not at least with traditional medicine or psychotherapy. Had we not intervened, you could compromise your mental health permanently, and that was something we didn't want to risk. Particularly, Gloria wasn't ready to lose you forever."

Dave turned his glance to Gloria, and she sighed. "James, we always liked each other since the first day we met, but with time, our feelings became stronger, and we started dating. In the beginning, it was something we preferred to keep secret because of the nature of our jobs, but something you cannot command is the heart, so we dated openly. If that accident didn't happen, we would have been married within a year." Her voice flickered, and she took a pause as her eyes shone with tears.

"Well, things never go the way you hope, do they?"

"Was this the reason why I felt attracted to you since the first moment? But then what happened?" He couldn't yet believe them, mainly because he should have remembered at least something of his past.

Nevertheless, he was also intrigued to understand how or whether this had been possible.

"We elaborated a procedure to help those agents who suffer from a severe nervous breakdown; it's a way to protect them until they can fully recover from the shock. Our labs developed a microchip which, once inserted in your brain, can override your memories with simulated ones." His voice turned into a monotone tune.

"You received a brand-new identity, name, and personality. We gave you a job suitable for the recovery period. Therefore, from the brave, highly military-trained James Eldings, you became the dull, shy, invisible Dave Stanford. We provided you with a job as an editor at the local newspaper.

"You were surrounded by our agents who had the task of keeping an eye on you. People like your employer, your doctor, the superintendent of the building you lived in, and so on. Your brain needed to recover, and meanwhile, your dull life was offering the quiet you required. Your doctor was prescribing you the medications to prepare your mind to cope with the trauma and making you ready to regain your identity," Dr. Nielsen kept his eyes steadily locked into Dave's.

"So, do you think now I'm recovered?" Dave shook his head, glancing at the people surrounding him.

"We believe so, but confirmation will be obtained once the microchip is deactivated and your identity restored. Another reason to bring you back was a suspected malfunction in the chip, and we feared you started to remember on an unconscious level too." Anton added. "During the nights, you returned to kill those who acted unjustly against people you considered innocent. Perhaps it was a way your subconscious wanted to clear his responsibility or wanted to give us a warning about your readiness to come back into action. We will bring back all the memories and allow you to return to be the one you have been born to be.

"However, concerning the possibility of you returning to be operational, it's still a question mark." Anton stood up, walking to get some water from the table in the middle of the room.

At that point, he really couldn't trust a word of what they said. That belonged to a sci-fi movie, and last time he checked, he was living in the real world.

"You certainly don't mean to say that I'm the avenger!"

"Yes, it was you," Gloria admitted, "and this is the reason why I had to leave. We were afraid it was because of my presence that you became the night avenger. We needed to see whether, without me, you would continue to kill those criminals or not. It was when we realized this was not going to stop you, and particularly that you were in danger, we decided to act fast and have you back."

CHAPTER 13

Dave's head spun, like the rest of the room around him.

For once, he was grateful to be already seated, or he would have collapsed on the floor.

"All my memories... everything I recall about my youth is something you recreated artificially?" he mumbled.

He took a couple of moments to understand the meaning of their words and the consequences in his life.

Recollecting his composure, he glared at Dr. Nielsen. "Did you ask me whether I wanted this or not?" His voice raised in the quiet of the room.

"Yes, this was agreed between you and us. You were fully aware of what would happen to you, and you haven't been the only one to have been under this treatment. At the time, you had only two choices, either you would accept this period of recovery or you would have risked ending up in a mental hospital for the rest of your life. I guess the first one was a better option, and this was the reason why we both agreed to it," Anton went on calmly, drinking his glass of water.

Dave stood and paced around, like a beast in a cage, bringing his hands to his head as if to keep it from exploding.

Thoughts swirled confusedly in his brain, memories, places, people. An overexcited state of mind overwhelmed him, impeding any clear view.

Stopping in the center of the room he turned himself to face the other three people present and felt like a puppy lost in the darkness.

He glanced at the door, considering the possibility of running away from that madness, but rationality told him to stay until the situation was clarified.

After another long pause, he shook his head. "I don't believe I would have ever agreed upon this kind of deal... You're lying to me!" Dave yelled, pointing his finger at them.

"We were expecting you to say something like this. For this reason, we recorded the whole meeting we had," Dr. Nielsen grabbed a remote control.

He pushed a button and the sizable display on the other side of the wall started up.

Anton stood and walked carefully toward him like he was approaching a wild beast. "Please come and take a seat. We understand this isn't something easy for you, but we're here to help. In the next days, all your memories will be returned to you, together with your real identity," Anton added, gently guiding him to the couch.

Curiosity won over the rage, taking the side of rationality in his mind, suggesting to, at least, listen to what they had to say and try to judge things with maximum care.

He walked to the couch and without saying another word, he sat down. As the recording started, he recognized his younger self, without any shadow of a doubt, but his eyes were red, swollen by tears, and obviously he hadn't slept in days.

His hands were shaking and his hair messy.

Dr. Nielsen was seated at a desk in front of him, his expression grave as he scrutinized James.

"How are you, today?" he asked, keeping his gaze straight on him.

"It was me who was supposed to die. I killed one of my best friends... I can't go over what happened." His voice was barely audible as it came out as a disconnected whimper.

"James, we're quite concerned about your health. You cannot continue being on duty, and I hope this is something that you can also agree with. You're not in the condition to take on any task at all."

His voice was calm, and he talked slowly, making sure he would understand every single word he spoke.

James nodded as tears started flowing from his eyes. "What am I supposed to do? I can't live this way. I don't want to go on with my life like this... I thought time would help me to overcome this desperate sorrow I'm experiencing, and with the therapy I've followed, I was sure I would have been able to cope with my mistakes..."

James took a short pause, closing his eyes as his fingers twisted with each other. "It's been two months since the accident, and I can't forgive myself; the nightmares I continue to see at night... Please help me."

"We might try one last thing to get you back from this state..." Dr. Nielsen proposed. James raised his glance to look at him.

"Do you mean the same sort of treatment Sandra had?"

"Yes, her recovery was almost miraculous, and she returned to her duties after two years. Now, I cannot predict how much time it will take for you to recover, but it's a solution worth trying. We will give you a new identity, a new job, a new life. You will be followed and monitored constantly by those who will be around you. You will never acknowledge their identity, as they will be perhaps your employer, your doctor, the landlord, and so on. Your real personality will be kept dormant and everything you will remember are the false memories the microchip we will apply is going to override. In your new identity, your brain will have the time to recover, and when we're sure you can return to yourself, we will have you back," Dr. Nielsen explained the procedure, the flicker in his voice betraying the tension in his soul.

"What kind of life will I have?"

"Considering the gravity of your situation, it must be a quite uneventful and dull life; believe me, you will need it." James sighed and lowered his gaze, remaining silent for a moment to think about it.

He then raised his glance and tried to smile. "Yes, I can't see any other solution. This pain has to stop. I-I need help, and this seems to be an acceptable compromise. Whether it will take two or more years of my life, it will always be better than having it totally ruined forever." His voice was a broken whisper, between the tears and moans.

Sensing the depth of his sorrow, tears shone like diamonds in his eyes. Never in his life could he have fathomed the emotional breakdown leading a man to withdraw almost entirely from his own life to avoid insanity.

The recording stopped, and the whole room remained immersed in silence. Everybody was waiting for Dave to say something, although they were aware it wasn't easy to understand.

The coming back was one of the most critical moments, and it could happen successfully only when the patient was fully aware of the deal. "I need some time to digest it. Do I need to have my memories back right away?" Dave wondered.

"No. No need to rush, and perhaps it would be a brilliant idea if you will stay here at the headquarters for some time before returning to your own identity," Anton explained.

"Gloria can help you with this. What do you think?" He turned his glance to her and then to Dr. Nielsen, who nodded thoughtfully, considering the best approach. "I think it's a great idea. We can go through a series of psychotherapy sessions to help you digest the news you had and will prepare you for the day when your identity will be fully restored. Gloria will support you emotionally, as she has always been by your side."

With a bright smile, she stood from the couch and gently took his hand in hers. The warmth of her touch melted the fear in his soul and gave him new hope for the future.

He wasn't thinking about the gangsters who were planning to eliminate him anymore. Most likely he would never have to see them again.

"I can show you your room," Gloria proposed.

"I don't have any of my clothes with me. Everything I have is in the apartment where I was living," Dave protested weakly, still dumbfounded at the revelation about his real identity.

"You still have all the clothes you used before. All your belongings have been brought here, so you don't need anything of what is there in the apartment. Nevertheless, we're going to send someone to pack everything and empty the place. You will have everything tomorrow afternoon," Anton assured.

"What about the coat and fedora I had in my closet? What's their meaning? Why do I have them?" Dave wondered. Indeed, it didn't belong to his grandfather as he recalled.

"That is a sort of uniform we have. It's something to distinguish our members. It gives a touch of style, doesn't it? You asked to have it because you liked it, so we made you believe it belonged to your grandfather," Dr. Nielsen explained.

"Everything I remember was made up? How?" Dave turned to face them once again.

"On second thought, I'm not sure I want to know. Forget it. One thing I would like to know though is this: If I wouldn't have started killing those people during the night, would you have brought me back now? How much time was I supposed to remain in my fake life?"

"We'd already discussed the possibility, and we aimed to bring you back in the following months anyway. You sent us into a rush." Anton's relaxed voice seemed almost to contrast with what he was saying. "Perhaps it was a signal that you were finally ready to return, and we should have been a bit less cautious in our decision. Nevertheless, I want you to understand that everything we did was to help you.

"We're a small group, but we do look after each other. People are not a commodity. There are many reasons for our wish to care about our members. One of them is because of their uncommon fighting, problem-solving, and reliability skills. The other is because, with time, we become like a sort of family, and we do everything to help each other.

"A government organization would have slammed you in a mental facility, searching for a better replacement; we don't do that," Anton reassured.

Dave nodded without saying a word. "What kind of institution is this?"

Standing from the couch, Anton strolled toward him, extracting a pack of cigarettes from his pocket.

"We're a group of military-trained professionals coming from different backgrounds. Many of us came from the French Foreign Legion; others are former UK SF, and so on.

"People are not chosen only because of their training, but also based on organizational, leadership, and strategical skills. Our staff is made up of highly educated people who can understand how to work in other countries and deal with different cultures." He patted Dave's shoulder in a friendly manner.

"We're recruited as mercenary forces not only during military actions, we cooperate with the intelligence of many other nations supporting their personnel or training their new recruits. This is not Hollywood bullshit, we're real," he added, walking away toward the garden to light his cigarette.

"I think I need some time to digest everything, and I need to be alone," Dave concurred. "Can you show me the place so I can get familiar with it?" He glanced at Gloria.

"Of course, come." She grabbed his hand, and without anything else left to say, they walked out of the room, followed by the scrutinizing glance of Dr. Nielsen.

The touch of Gloria's hand reassured and soothed his soul. Perhaps things are not going that badly.

If this is my life, I think it will be far better than the one I was living before. The only question I have is whether once I regain my identity and memories, will I be any different, or will I remember anything about what happened during those five years?

Gloria perceived his confusion and guessed his discomfort by the way he squeezed her hand. "What's on your mind?" she asked gently.

"Everything is so confusing," he tried to explain. "What kind of man is James? Is he different from the person I am now?"

"Not at all. The only difference is that, well, he's less clumsy, but still the same good-hearted, thoughtful, and deep person you are. The new personality was aimed to suppress some sides of your character, but the main traits of your nature remained. What changed were the memories and the path of life. Certainly, those factors influence the behavior, but not completely.

"Perhaps you should have a chat with Sandra; she also went through your same experience, and she can give you her point of view."

"So, I'm not the clumsy, shy virgin guy..." His gaze lowered as if he regretted asking about his personal life.

"No, you're not. You are a bit reserved, but certainly not a virgin," Gloria giggled.

"You said we were dating and considering getting married... I was attracted to you from the first moment you came into my life, but I can't say this is love. Will my feelings change once my identity is restored?"

Coping with a relationship he couldn't remember was something he'd never fathomed as possible. It was all too surreal to believe, and the fear of having something ruined didn't appeal to him.

"Yes, we were dating. I still love you the way I always used to, and God only knows how I have been missing you. But I knew this was for your own good, so I was patiently waiting for you to return. I don't know whether once you are back, our relationship will suffer and will be changed into a friendly one, but I'm still happy to have you close." Her green eyes, steady on his, flickered with a melancholic light.

Although she tried to reassure him that even being friends would be enough for her, he sensed that wasn't corresponding to what she wanted.

With a shy smile, he acknowledged his feelings toward Gloria were reserved only for one person in the world.

Yet, she was right, and nobody could forecast what their relationship would be once he was back to his real self.

Only time can tell, he thought.

"Here is your room," she opened a door.

He walked inside and looked around at the decorations on the walls and the paintings on the ceiling.

Every detail, from the living space beside the windows where two armchairs were placed at the side of a sofa table, to the impressive fireplace ready to warm the winter nights.

The elaborate afghan carpets decorating the dark wooden floor gave a final touch to the image.

"I think I have never seen anything like this, except for the pictures in the magazines. Do we all live here, or is this used as a headquarters?"

"This is our choice." She walked toward the door to the balcony to give some fresh air to the environment. "We can choose to stay here or to have another personal residence, particularly when we prefer to have our own privacy, or we decide to have a family. Although this place could host the families of all the members, most of us like to use this place as a refuge when we come back from a mission. Here we get debriefed and ready to return to our lives. Come to see the panorama from here," she called.

Dave walked to the balcony and was amazed by the view of the woods surrounding the property. "What about me? Or what about us?"

Gloria glanced at him, not understanding the question. "What do you mean?"

"Well, did we have our own house, did we live here, or did we have separate houses?" He wished to hold her in his arms, but used all his determination to refrain from doing it.

Although this would have been considered normal behavior, the circumstances were bizarre enough to make him reconsider his actions.

"We both have our own apartments in the city; nothing as fancy as this villa, but we can afford something better than the one you were used to. The kind of risks we're taking on our missions makes our salaries higher than the average, so be reassured that the quality of your life is going to improve."

"Do you think I can go to see my place?" Dave wondered, interested in knowing everything about James' life.

"Better not. You should take back your life step by step and try not to rush. I know you are curious to discover yourself, but it's advisable to follow the procedure developed by Dr. Nielsen," she explained.

"I think I need to be alone. I need to think..."

"Of course," she handed him a mobile phone. "This is for you. Whenever you need any one of us, you just call, okay? I'll be around."

Dave grabbed the telephone and placed it in the pocket of his jeans. "Thanks, I'll let you know if I need anything."

With a quick kiss on his cheek, she rushed to exit the door, avoiding seeing his reaction to that. When he was alone, he went to check the wardrobe.

"I believe you can tell a lot about a person from the dress style," he considered aloud, opening a door he thought would have led to the walk-in closet.

He switched on the light and found himself in a spacious room; however, despite its size, there weren't many clothes. "I guess I have always been a sort of minimalist person, but I have style. Here there is the attire for many occasions, but mostly casual. I'm not that different from James, and Gloria might be right; my personality wasn't changed dramatically." He chose a shirt and jeans before deciding to go for a shower. He needed to relax and clean up his mind, and a long shower would be a good starting point.

***

From the morning after, his days were filled with psychotherapy sessions to prepare his brain for the recovery of the lost memories, together with a reintroduction to his life with Gloria.

James was no more a stranger, and as time went by, he began to identify more and more with him rather than with Dave.

He knew that was a fake identity and deserved to be left behind to give space to his reality.

Coping with the idea of being the reason why an agent was dead was perhaps the hardest part, but without these preparatory sessions and knowledge, Dr. Nielsen knew it meant just bringing him back to the middle of the same emotional storm that forced them to reach the decision of assigning him a new identity.

"Are you ready to return to your life?" Dr. Nielsen asked after one of the psychotherapy sessions.

The results he obtained were promising, and he was sure the time was right to commence the process of disabling the microchip, reinstating in full his memories and personality.

The uncertainty factor wasn't to be underestimated, and even though there was a good chance for the therapy to reveal itself as a success, the possibility of having him lost forever wasn't unfeasible.

There wasn't any hurry for Dave to return to be James, but the microchip was not developed to last forever, and sooner or later it was going to deactivate.

Before long, he would have to cope with his memories and feelings all at once, Dr. Nielsen considered with a grimace twisting his expression into a painful mask. He wasn't ready for such a risk.

"We will never know until I get it back, I guess," James smiled uncertainly, glancing at him. They were alone in the laboratory, where everything was ready for the process.

"Then, we can start..." He toughened his expression, preparing himself for one of the most demanding routines in his career as a psychiatrist.

For Gloria and Anton, who waited in another wing of the mansion, the wait was almost excruciating. Other members of the team were deployed in several locations abroad, taking care of the ongoing projects, and they were the only guests of the villa together with Dr. Nielsen and James.

The uncertainty of the results in bringing him back was killing Gloria, and she could not remain seated waiting for the result.

Every two minutes she stood, walking around, checking the clock and the telephone. Also, Anton, who generally was the one who had a hold of his emotions, couldn't hide the tension in his emotions.

Between the people of the organization, there were close friendships, and losing one of their members was an unspeakable pain, particularly when this happened during a mission.

The memory of the treatment Sandra went through returned to Gloria's mind, and she tried to be comforted by its favorable outcome, but this time there was more at stake.

There was her future with the man she loved more than everything else. "You'd better try to calm down," Anton warned calmly, reaching her with a soothing voice.

"Don't you think that I'm trying already? The uncertainty of what is going on inside that room is killing me," she glanced around, caught between the desire to reach the door of the lab and wait outside and the need to be as far as possible from it.

Anton stood from the chair, walking toward her. He held her tightly in his arms. "Come on, Gloria, you need to be strong and to trust Dr. Nielsen. There isn't anyone who would help James better than he can, and he will certainly bring back your boyfriend. Then one day you will marry and will have ten children..."

She parted from him with a grimace perturbing the beautiful features of her face. "Ten kids?? Not even one of those things!"

Anton laughed heartily. "Yep, that's the beauty in you, Gloria. You're the frankest person I've ever met, and never in this world will people hear anything nice from you if it's not matching exactly what you hold in your heart."

She smirked.

"How about if we go to have a cup of coffee? We will have fresh-baked croissants, and by the time we're back, James will get out from that room ready to embrace his old life," he proposed, guiding her toward the door.

She let him guide her, but when they were almost out, she glanced back once more at the place they came from and in the direction of the lab where Dr. Nielsen was locked.

Biting her lips, she hesitated.

Anton turned her back toward the kitchen. "Now-now, let's go," he whispered. "Now, my dear, I will show you how in France we make a perfect breakfast. My café au lait is something I am famous for, and since we have the tastier croissant bought every morning from the finest patisserie in town, you could fool yourself into thinking you've been brought to a lovely cafeteria in Marseilles."

He moved a chair from the table to allow her to have a seat, so he could provide her the best service.

Gloria still felt butterflies in her stomach, but he was the kind of guy who could make a woman forget about every trouble, and in that precise moment that was exactly what she needed.

After a couple of minutes, he returned carrying two large cups, which he placed on the table, and left once again to bring her the croissants. "Now, have a sip and tell me what you think."

A charming smile appeared on his face, trying to distract her attention from the stress of the wait.

She brought the cup to her lips, glancing at Anton already enjoying his creation. Her eyes opened wide as the full and rich flavor of what she considered purely heavenly filled her mouth.

"That is the best café au lait I have ever experienced. You're in the wrong business; you should be a barista, maestro." An amused chuckle escaped him as he placed his cup on the table.

"When I retire from this group, I'll think about the suggestion, or perhaps I'll move to a lovely location back in France and enjoy my time, getting as bored as possible."

She laughed as the tension untied and the knot in her stomach disappeared. "Thanks, I needed it."

"What are friends for?" After the coffee, Gloria and Anton returned to the meeting room where they were waiting for any news about James.

As nobody was yet there, they assumed Dr. Nielsen was still in the lab. She couldn't recall how much time it took for Sandra to complete the process, but she was sure it was going to take longer than her nerves could bear.

Standing, pacing, and returning to sit on the couch became an unnerving exercise, until the door opened and Dr. Nielsen appeared.

His eyes were swollen, and he held himself against the wall, fearing tiredness would have won over his determination, and he would fall onto the floor.

His face looked like he'd lost at least ten years of his life, but he was smiling.

"How is he doing?" Distressed, she turned to him.

"The patient needs absolute relaxation and solitude for the rest of the day. He's sedated and I'll keep an eye on him constantly. Regardless, the procedure was perfectly successful. I decided to take away some emphasis on the accident. There is no need for him to recall everything, and I would be glad if none of you would go chewing on old issues. The past cannot be undone, but we can reshape our future, so let's make it better," Dr. Nielsen warned as he took a seat in a chair.

Gloria felt her knees unable to sustain her anymore, relieved and euphoric at the same time. "Thank you, but now you too need to have some sleep, or soon we will need to have you going through the same treatment."

Dr. Nielsen nodded and grabbed the mobile phone. He called for a couple of assistants to help him to bring James back to his room, where he could lie down for as long as he needed.

Gloria observed them bringing him away without even the possibility of saying a single word. For her, nothing was worth mentioning and her feelings were too complex to even try to explain them to herself.

In the silence of her troubled soul, she also retired to her room and waited for the next day, trying to think about anything else.

Anton didn't even consider following her. He knew James and Gloria, from that moment on, would need some time to recover from the shock and regain their lives from the moment Dave returned to be James.

EPILOGUE

James' recovery took one entire month worth of guilt and forgiveness toward himself for the accident which cost the life of the one he considered one of his best friends.

Nevertheless, regaining his memories and reclaiming his life brought him the understanding of being where he belonged, to the place he was meant to be since he was born.

According to his physical and mental conditions, Dr. Nielsen ordered another two months before reinstating him to his duties.

During this time, he would carry out desk duties, either from his home or from the mansion.

Taking part in more demanding operations required some time which still needed to be assessed.

Going through his files also revealed the dark side of the tasks he accomplished. Most of them were connected with coldblooded assassinations, and it didn't quite matter whether those murdered people were considered terrorists.

His detached experience as Dave, the shy editor, gave him a broader perspective, and perhaps those dangerous people still had families and loved ones.

Many things in the back of his mind needed to be figured out, and mostly they had to do with reorganizing his own life and priorities.

"Will I return to be the same killing machine I was known to be?" His voice sounded in the stillness of his apartment.

He raised his gaze toward the window as the clock ticked noon.

The answer to his question wasn't easy, but being a mercenary soldier was part of his fiber, and if there was something he couldn't deny, that was his nature.

Yet, another issue kept his mind busy: the implications of how those years of being Dave affected his relationship with Gloria.

Having her back in his life, regaining and strengthening the bond which brought them together, was another benefit gifted by those five years' therapy.

Taking the reins of his identity meant also returning to his apartment, going through his belongings, memories, personal items he'd accumulated during his missions as a memento of the past years and a warning for the future to come.

He used his recovery time to go through every single item holding a special memory to keep forever.

A treasure hunt was the way he described it. He walked to the calendar he kept hanging on the wall.

March was reaching its end, and soon Spring would transform into Summer.

From the windows of the studio in his apartment, the view of the city brought a smile to his face.

Turning to return to his desk, his glance was captured by the coat and fedora carefully hanging on the hook at the entrance he spotted from the open door.

Like responding to a call, he strolled toward it and raised his hand to caress the soft fabric.

His mind was brought back to the time he called himself Dave, when the touch of the coat returned the memories of his grandfather.

He was aware they were a false reminiscence, but the sensations they gave him were real, and he aimed to treasure them in his heart.

As his hand unhurriedly ran along the length of the coat, he reached the pockets and a slight irregularity in it caused an almost imperceptible cringe on his face.

Yet, curious to understand what created the bulge, he searched the pocket. From its inside, a folded sheet of paper appeared.

Surprise left him open-mouthed, as unfolding it, he recognized the drawing Gloria chose to have for herself – the man walking on a misty day.

The man from the mist... He shook his head.

Perhaps this is the place where a person like me belongs. I'm not a man who lives in the sunshine; I live and work in the secrecy of the haze.

That consideration brought to his mind many questions that needed an answer.

Yet, maybe they were all in the drawing and the meaning of the silhouette strolling from the thick of the mist, as if he was created by it. Holding the sheet of paper, he reached the balcony and grabbed a chair.

He sat down, watching the afternoon sky. Leaving his thoughts free to run across his mind, he closed his eyes, enjoying the warmth of the afternoon sun.

Ultimately, a steady thought would have hit him, bringing the answer to solve all the questions forming in his head.

After an hour, or maybe more, he lost track of time, but like being struck by lightning, he jumped from his chair, rushed to grab his fedora and coat, and left the apartment.

Indeed, it wasn't the right weather for that attire, but he followed his instinct, maintaining his focus and purpose.

He reached his car, and keeping his thoughts focused on that thought, with his heart starting to beat faster and faster as the road went by, he had a glimpse of his final destination, the purpose for his existence unfolding in front of him. Parking the car in the yard before the mansion intimidated him.

The high walls almost seemed to have eyes and all glanced at him from the past, curious to understand what his intentions were.

Toughening his expression, he strode toward the entrance. He was confident he would have found all the people to whom he needed to announce his decision gathered in the large working room.

His heart raced as he reached the second floor, and clenching his fists, he entered the room wearing his best smile. Gloria, Anton, Dr. Nielsen, and the chief of operations, Aileen McAngus, were discussing something about the next mission, when suddenly the door opened and uninvited, James irrupted like fury.

"Good afternoon, ladies and gentlemen," he greeted, glancing at each of the people present in the room, reserving the widest smile for Gloria.

She was the one included in the plan swirling in his mind.

"I thought you were still taking some time for your recovery. How are you doing?" Aileen asked, surprised to see him arrive.

"I started getting bored, and I think I'm ready to come back into action." He paced to the table and took a seat, hoping to find the right words to explain what was haunting his thoughts. "However, I had the time not only to recover fully, but also to reconsider myself."

With a short pause to ensure he had their full attention, he continued. "My life has gone through dramatic changes, and the last five years have perhaps taught me something about myself that I've ignored. Most of all, I've learned where my place is, the one from where I need to act. I understand it's difficult to explain the situation to you, and this sort of enlightening arrived as a surprise while I was enjoying the fair day on my balcony." He looked around. "And you, too, will be surprised, I believe."

"Then you only have to keep blurting out everything that's in your heart and then wait to find out whether we can figure out anything. If we have questions, we will ask." Anton scrutinized him through narrowed eyelids, with his usual half-smile to make people understand he knew what they were up to, but he was waiting for them to reveal their plan.

"This is perhaps the best solution," James approved. "I mean to partially withdraw from the operation and become a sort of occasional player. This has nothing to do with what happened in the past, but rather it's about the way I want to shape my future."

From his coat's pocket, he took out the drawing he made and unfolded it on the table in front of them. "When I made the drawing Gloria brought with her, I thought I was inspired by the things that started to happen in my life. Today, when I accidentally found the sketch again, everything was clear in my mind. I wasn't influenced by the situation I was living in at the moment. Rather, it was a message from my subconscious about what I want and what I need."

"Hold on a moment," Aileen interrupted, her face turning severe at the possibility of losing one of her best resources. "Are you trying to tell us you mean to quit?"

"No, not really. I don't want to resign totally. I want to step aside a little, like the shadows in the mist that appear to our eyes only when we look at them. I'll be available whenever you require me, but officially, I'm going to set up for partial retirement." He stood glancing at the surprised faces of those who still didn't quite grasp what he meant to do.

Then, he glanced at Gloria. "If you want to disappear in the mist with me, we can be happy together, have more time for ourselves and our lives, and yet be available whenever you require," he reached his hand to her.

Gloria opened up into a bright smile and walked toward him. "Count me in," she whispered without thinking about it, because she knew following her heart meant making sure she would not lose him another time.

Dr. Nielsen remained silent the whole time. He was analyzing the situation and gently rubbing his chin with his hand. He understood this would be the best solution, not only for the top agent they had, but also for the future of a newborn couple who deserved some happiness after the storm raging in their lives.

"That's it?" Anton wondered, surprised.

"Yep," Gloria beamed, like she grasped perfectly what James meant. "When you need us, find us in the mist..."

Without waiting for a reply, they both walked away, and as the sun started to set on the fields in the countryside, and the slight evening haze began to rise, James and Gloria disappeared... back to the mist.

ONE LAST THING...

If you enjoyed this book or if you found it useful, I'd be very grateful if you'd post a short review on Amazon. Your support really does make a difference.

Thanks again for your help!

ABOUT THE AUTHOR

Hello! This is the end of the book, I hope you enjoyed it.

I was born in 1973 in a small town in Italy. In my career, I've edited and wrote several scientific papers on geology and engineering, with emphasis on final disposal for spent nuclear waste. However, I come from a very complex background. I graduated from the Art Institute of Perugia (Italy) but pursued further studies in geosciences and environmental geosciences. I am passionate about photography, and I love observing nature and human's societies from every perspective.

Through my novels, I aim to propose a new way to look at human relationships, cultures, and beliefs.

You can find me also on Facebook:

https://www.facebook.com/paperpenandinkwell

https://www.facebook.com/PJ.Mann.paperpenandinkwell

Twitter:
https://twitter.com/PjMann2016
And of course, my website:
https://pjmann2016.wixsite.com/pjmann

Made in the USA
Coppell, TX
23 August 2021